A HAPPY BUREAUCRACY

Nothing is certain, but atomic death and taxes.

M.P. FITZGERALD

Gonzo Fiction

The author greatly appreciates you taking the time to read his work. Please
consider leaving a review wherever you bought the book, or telling your
friends about it to help us spread the word.

Thank you for supporting my work.

 Created with Vellum

For my mother, who overpaid her taxes by a dollar so that the IRS would have to spend more money in postage, labor, and paper to refund it to her.

Author's note: Strewn between drug use, groin malice, and cursing on a level tantamount to sacrilege, are gratuitous mentions of bureaucracy. These bureaucratic references may not be for the weak of heart.

PROLOGUE

Stifled breath was held as an offense was made on the door. There was nothing here but dust and radiation, and the cold glare from an uncaring sun. There was supposed to be no one living for miles, he had made sure of that. Yet blows rattled the door in quick succession. The word 'knocking' was not in his vocabulary, because no one had knocked since The War. He did not dare let out his breath, but realized a fraction too late that she, the little girl with a knife to her throat, had begun to cry.

Whoever was on the other side of the door would hear her. The option to hide had gone.

"Fuck," he whispered at the child. Her whimpers were not loud, but when silence is the natural order, even a sneeze from a mouse would sound like blaring klaxons. He put down the butcher's knife onto his table and the little girl's eyes spelled relief. He replaced the knife with his rusty hunting rifle. Fight or flight were now having their familiar debate inside of him, and before either could win another blow came at the door.

"Hello?" a meek voice said through the door. "Do you have a moment?"

What is this? the man thought, uncertain if there was any danger. Instinct won over indecisiveness and he loaded an ancient bullet into the gun's chamber.

"Hello?"the little girl whimpered.

"Yes, hello? Do you have time to talk?" the voice asked politely. "It is very important."

Slavers kick in the door; raiders wait until you are outside. This, well, this was confusing. So, with the affront to his brain winning, and the option of surprise gone, the man opened the door.

Outside there was dust, and then there was irradiated dust. What was once a thriving and happy suburb, a perfect portrait of the American dream, was now a dead nightmare. The hydrogen bombs never made it this far, but their wrath spread without impetus. The War had ended modern history, and it started something that would make the dark ages look like a regular renaissance. The houses that were once built for families were now mostly empty, rotting slowly under a cruel sun. The grass that once grew on this house's lawn had dried up decades ago, and then burned for warmth. What were once windows were now a collection of boards nailed into the wall of the house haphazardly, their origin likely from the picket fences of the other houses; the people responsible for nailing them now long dead. What was outside was misery, misery and dust. There should be nothing else...

...Yet, there he was. Standing weaponless, and awkwardly, was a man who was somehow washed and clean shaven. His hair cut short and parted to the right, business like. His skin was somehow fair and not sun damaged to a tan leather. This man, against all odds, was wearing clothes that had not only been washed, but also ironed. His shirt collared and white, his shoes black polished and neatly tied. There was something around his neck; it should have been the bones of his enemies, strung through their dried tendons; it should have been a makeshift bandolier made of bullets and spikes, but instead it was a tie. A regular black tie, with a Windsor knot. Where there should be a club, a gun, or a spear in hand, was a clipboard and a pen.

The pen was not stabbed into someone's eyes, which was the only use he had ever witnessed seeing someone do with one. He had only ever seen someone who looked like this in photographs, before The War.

Standing in the distance, leaning on what was once a tree, was a man who did look like he belonged. Shotgun in hand, he was dressed in biker leathers and as rugged and miserable as the earth beneath him. This was professional protection. After making eye contact, he lowered his weapon. No one needed to die yet.

"Hello!" The man in the tie said "My name is Arthur McDowell, I am an agent of the Internal Revenue Services. And you are?"

"What?" the man responded.

"I am an agent for the IRS, I am here for an audit."

He had been warned about this. Of all of the gangs in the United Wastes, the IRS was the most powerful. He had never met an agent, but he had met others who had. The last time he had joined a raiding gang, the oldest of the group told him once that "there are only two for sure things in this world, death and taxes. The IRS wants only one of those, but they'll take *both* if you do not cooperate." Everything else he had heard sounded like myth or a horror story.

Arthur McDowell clicked the top of his pen tentatively, as dust from the dead planet beneath him shifted from wind. Arthur was now looking at the man inquisitively, and the man behind him in leather rested a single finger on his trigger. "Is this the residence of the 'Murder-Man?'" Arthur asked.

Someone talked. Someone gave him away. If anybody of his old gang had sold him out to slavers, torture would come before death once he got his paws on them, but if the stories about the IRS were true, he wasn't sure if he could even be mad. Hell, if the stories were true, he'd do the same.

"Yeah, I'm Murder-Man."

"Good," said Arthur, hurriedly writing something on his board. "Mr. Man, it seems that you did not do your taxes this season. Now, as the postal service has not delivered here in a generation we can understand the oversight. As an Auditor I am here to fix that."

"Oh", said Murder-Man, "what ah, what are taxes?"

"That is a surprisingly common question Mr. Man, so no need to be embarrassed."

He wasn't embarrassed at all, he was afraid. "Taxes are a percentage of your income that is mandatorily volunteered to the United States government for the goods and services provided to you, a citizen, and to keep the government running. It is our patriotic duty, and law, to pay them."

"Oh."

"It looks like you have not paid your taxes this season, Mr. Man, and though the IRS understands that this kind of omission is likely given the circumstances..." Arthur swept his hand around him, meaning 'circumstances' to be human holocaust by nuclear fire. "...they still must be paid." The man in the biker leathers stood upright at 'must be paid' and stepped a little closer. Murder-Man had no intention of pissing him off.

"How ah, how ya want me to pay 'em?" Murder-Man asked, not eloquently.

"With United States currency of course!"

"You want old world money?"

"Preferably, yes, but the IRS has positioned itself to work

with today's economy, so for your convenience we are willing to take bullets or calories."

This was the most polite raid Murder-Man had ever experienced.

Keeping his gun low, so as not to piss off the hired help, Murder-Man leaned on his doorframe, eyeing Arthur suspiciously. He was hoping the girl stayed quiet. "How much ya want?" he finally asked, after another moment filled with listless dust passed.

"That is what we are here to find out, Mr. Man, I know that you are unfamiliar with our process; again, nothing to be embarrassed about..." Arthur said to a man who was still not embarrassed. "...we do not take a set amount from everybody; we only take a percentage of your combined income and assets."

Murder-Man knew neither of those words, but it was the one that sounded more sexual that raised his interest. "What's a ass-set?" he asked.

"Oh! Why, those are the things you own! Let's go through those first. You own this house?"

"Yeah."

"Good, good," Arthur said, writing on his clipboard. He seemed to be enjoying himself. "Let's see, you are a homeowner, and according to your old gang, you were a raider by profession?" *Someone did talk!* Murder-Man's mind howled with rage. His words were muted, "Yeah. I don' do that no more."

Arthur did not look up at this, and his writing quickened. "Unemployed? That's a shame. Have you been jobless this whole season?" Not sure what Arthur meant by 'season' Murder-Man stared blankly and said "Yeah" just to hurry things along.

"It can be a very hostile job market in today's world that is for sure. Well, judging by the size of your house, and the fact that it is not radiated, we will classify it as class three. You should be very proud!"

"Uh, thank you?"

"Mmmm Hmmm..." Arthur replied, still laying his attention on the clipboard. "Assuming you can't pay with currency, that would put what you owe to be 80,000 calories, 150 bullets, or a combination of the two." Arthur reached into his pocket and fished out a calculator. "I can, of course, help you with the conversion."

Murder-Man's breathing was thin. Flight or fight had not been resolved.

"I, uh, I don't have that—" he started, before he was quickly interrupted by a now giddy Arthur.

"Wait, we haven't gone over your deductibles! The IRS is no armed robber sir," he declared, despite having an armed man behind him. "Do you have any dependents?"

"What's that?"

Before Arthur could answer the little girl stirred. Murder-Man had no time to retaliate, and before he could make a move to hide her, she was peeking out of the doorway. Her dirty bruised face that had only known fear and hunger looked out and onto Arthur's clean and studious one. It looked like children were not something Arthur saw often. They stared at each other with suspicion and disbelief. Arthur shifted his weight uneasily as his Enforcer, the hired help, moved forward.

"That," Arthur said, pointing at the little girl "is a dependent." He made a little check on his board.

Murder-Man thumbed back at the little girl, and his hanging jaw snapped back into place to speak. "My cow?" he asks.

"My mistake," Arthur replied, sullenly, understanding the term. "She's your calories," he continued, stating, not asking.

"Yeah, was gonna chop her and cook her before you

punched my door all polite like." A grin crept onto Murder-Man's face. The little girl had been 'taught' not to run, and even now, in the face of death she did not dare. She had been kept alive this long only so that her meat would be fresh when Murder-Man ran out of canned food.

"Can't say for certain until we get her to the headquarters and weigh her, but she looks to be around 90,000 calories. This would leave you with a refund of 10,000 calories which we'd mail to you within four to five weeks," Arthur said, hurriedly, still avoiding eye contact. He finished writing and presented the clipboard to Murder-Man. "Sign here."

Murder-Man did not understand the gesture, nor could he write or read. What he did understand though was that the men in front of him intended to rob him of his meal. A meal he had gone a great length to keeping alive this long and one that was only going to be eaten if he had no other food. The IRS was as confusing and frightening as he had heard. The man in leather could certainly kill him, but if they took his food, well, he would die slowly. The math was simple: starve, or go out fighting.

He cocked his gun.

CHAPTER ONE

Wood splinters flew into the air. Gun smoke ate at Arthur's lungs. Blood turned to mud. Then there was silence.

Arthur did what he always did when the person he was auditing inevitably raised their gun: he fell to the ground and covered his ears. He was incredibly quick at this. The trick was to fall backward, instead of forward or straight down. He learned this by memorizing the graphic they kept at the office next to the one about CPR and the Heimlich maneuver. It read: "Guns go up? Don't frown! Fall down!" and depicted the same placid looking art that all workplace cartoons had settled on. He was quietly repeating this to himself, a sort of mad mantra to ease the sudden trauma.

His Enforcer was a damn good shot and Murder-Man was right to fear him. He was named Murder-Man for a reason, however. There were now three bodies on the ground, but Arthur's was the only one that was going to get up and leave.

Murder-Man had murdered his last man.

The Enforcer had fired off two shots, both hits. The first one to kill Murder-Man, the second a revenge shot for being killed himself. Stray buckshot had nicked the doorframe from a house that would never be repaired. Murder-Man only fired off one shot, but it counted.

A display of malice splayed gruesomely across the dust. It was a picture of cruelty and indifference. It was the only kind of portrait that was ever painted in the United Wastes. Blood soaked through clothes from cooling bodies, the constant commentary running through their brains finally finished.

Time for paperwork.

Arthur could wait until he was safe at his office to write up a 22-B *Violent Incident in the Workplace* form; there was nothing in the manual that said he had to do it on site. But why put off for later what he can do now? He had the forms with him (this was of course, not the first time this had happened, by any means) and the scene was still fresh in his mind. Taking a moment to dust himself off and straighten his tie, Arthur McDowell started checking off boxes.

"Right," Arthur declared aloud "Two dead, one taxpayer, one Enforcer. Very unfortunate." His handwriting was mindless, the form was being filled out by muscle memory. He drew out a slab of sticky notes from his pants' pocket, placed one on the completed 22-B and wrote *Memo to self, send condolences and flowers to Robert's family.* He hummed as he worked.

When the bombs fell and the weather forecast became permanent nuclear fire, and when flowers of destructive fusion blossomed, leaving death in their wake, the least important question was immediately asked: *Who is going to collect all of the taxes?* It was, without doubt, bureaucracy's greatest triumph, next to the ticketed queue of course.

The Internal Revenue Services were well prepared for The War. Yes, it came as a surprise, but the preparation had been done nearly a generation prior. The National Emergency Operations Manual was updated in the 1980s with a contingency for nuclear war. Taxes were to be collected 30 days after the Holocaust, and that is exactly what happened. Bunkers were built beneath the surface and the IRS had its own nuclear shelter. They were not the only American institution to have these bunkers - the paranoia of the cold war made sure that they were as standard as electric heating - but they were the only ones to survive. The only people on the planet who took safety drills seriously were fire marshals and bureaucrats. So when the alarms went off, and eyes rolled because of another drill, it was the IRS with their inhuman bureaucratic standards and observation of rules that made it out alive.

To be clear: the newly revised National Emergency Operations Manual that was in circulation when the bombs fell did not contain information on how to rebuild society. It did, however, carry information detailing which institutions should be prioritized in receiving taxes so *they* could rebuild. Frankly, it just wasn't the IRS's department, and it wasn't their fault that the other parts of the government didn't have their shit together. Thirty days after Oppenheimer's gift killed the planet, a census of the immediate population was taken. The manual declared that anyone, no matter their position, rank or function could be reassigned to census taking in an emergency. Once there was a head count, the auditing and the collection of taxes began. So, taxes were collected, and the stores of the IRS grew fat because there was no one for them to distribute to. It was the first time in generations that there was a surplus in the federal budget.

Arthur McDowell was a second generation Auditor.

His father was a janitor before The War and was conscripted into census taking twice. The second census killed him. Now, Arthur McDowell stood in a dead wasteland, the United Wastes of America as the pride and joy of the IRS. He was efficient, did everything by the letter and, most importantly, he was a true believer.

Though the scene around him was grim there was a pep in his step. With the collection of today's audit, Arthur

McDowell was finished with his year's quota, and he was finished early. *They will have to promote me now*, he thought with glee as he sidestepped the mangled flesh of a man named 'Murder'. *I can have my own office, and be safe from all of this. I can finally be safe.*

Standing a few feet away, paralyzed with fear, was the little girl. Once a 'Cow', to be eaten as a last resort, she was now a payment to the IRS. The title made no difference; she had been a commodity her entire life. What she didn't know was that the IRS did not distinguish value from its calorie payments whether it was dead or alive. What she didn't know was that it was within her captor's right to slice off the over-payment of 10,000 calories and keep it. What she didn't know was that Arthur was probably the first man who cared if she died.

He might have been a bureaucrat, and he might have been living in a world where it was every man for himself, where the consequences of failure were often cannibalism, but he was no monster.

Arthur did his best to smile at the little girl, a gesture which did not come off as natural, and too late he realized that the little girl had likely only ever seen a grown man smile when he was doing something violent. She winced, but did not move. Arthur did not have the skills set to talk to children.

"Some ah, some weather we got, don't we?" Arthur stammered. It was a good topic around the water rations, sure to get anyone complaining.

Silence.

Arthur started to fret. *I don't know how to talk to her,* he thought, the bodies below him now as cold as the wind. *I don't want to sound condescending, but I also don't want to pander.* Tears formed in the child's eyes. This just made Arthur fret more.

"You're safe now little girl, I'm from the government. Do

you understand 'safe'?" She shook her head. "Do you understand 'government'?" She shook her head again.

He, like the rest of the country, was used to death. Though he didn't like it, he was accustomed to being around cadavers. Cruelty is so par for the course in the United Wastes, his heart should be calloused. Yet, it was breaking.

Arthur placed his pen under the metal clip on his board, and with his free hand gently held the hand of the little girl. She winced, but made no attempt to fight him. Arthur led her out of the once more abandoned house. Within a few steps, they were past Robert's body. A few more and they were on the cracked pavement of the street.

The road was littered with the remains of panic. Cars that will never run again sat with their doors open, like stranded whales with their flippers splayed out. They were all empty, though they may have been stuffed to the brim before scavengers found them. Suitcases lived on the road, empty like oysters picked clean. The world was a graveyard for all of humankind's now useless things. As Arthur and the silent girl trudged across the street, random bits of plastic, eroded to unrecognizable shapes, crunched beneath their feet.

"Looks like the sanitation department has a lot of work to do," Arthur stated in a half jest, half whine, and without thinking stated the unofficial motto of bureaucracy – "oh well, not my department." The little girl said nothing.

There was no more sanitation department.

The little girl stopped, letting what small weight she had pull against Arthur's stride. When she had his attention, she looked up at him with urgency. "We don' have a gun," she said. She may not know the words 'government' or 'safe' but she knew the rules of the United Wastes: kill or be killed, or kill or be raped, then killed, then partially eaten, then worn as a trophy. Whichever came first, naturally.

"Gun? No-no-no, *he* has the gun," Arthur stated, pointing

at what was once Robert (his Enforcer). "He has the gun so that I can audit." The little girl's worries were clearly not eased, but she pulled out her anchors and continued to walk. The lesson she appeared to have learned from him was that he was *crazy*.

They trekked on.

Arthur led her in silence, four blocks down where the roads were no longer packed with derelict cars. There he took her to the only running vehicle in miles, a government-issued white IRS minivan. Though the undercarriage of the van was as dusty as the earth, the rest of it was spotless, having been washed just before being leased to Arthur and Robert. Painted on one side was a round blue circle encasing a gold badge with a weighing scale and key in the center. The words around the circle read *The Department of the Treasury* Internal Revenue Services*. Arthur had hand washed this part of the van. And so, in the first time in history, a strange man led a little girl to a white van and nothing bad happened to her.

Realizing that the little girl had likely never been inside a vehicle that could run, Arthur buckled her in and started the motor. He adjusted his own seat, checked his mirrors, and turned on his left blinker. Instead of immediately heading to the IRS headquarters, he decided to drive back to Murder-Man's house. The little girl's mood changed slightly as the van moved; she looked unfamiliar with the sensation, though it should never be so foreign to a child. *Had she never experienced fun?* Arthur thought.

"What's, ah, what's your name?" he asked.

"Dinner."

Of course it was.

Arthur slowly weaved the van between the derelict cars, a task that Robert had avoided. It took longer than he had any patience for, but it was something he had to do. Ten minutes passed before he successfully navigated his way the four blocks to the house. "This will only take a couple minutes. Is there anything you want to get while we are here?" asked Arthur. With determination in her eyes, Dinner nodded, jumped out of the van and ran into the house. With a heavy heart, Arthur left the van and opened its back door. He looked at Robert, now just meat.

"I'm sorry," he said.

Then with much labor, he dragged the heavy body into the back of the van.

Soon, Dinner emerged from the house, clutching the cleaver that was held to her throat only a short time ago. She held its sharp edge at face level. *Is this why she asked if I had a gun?* Arthur panicked. The little girl knelt down to Murder-Man's corpse, and with a single, purposeful motion, she hacked off one of his fingers. It bled very little. Arthur was surprised by her efficiency, as he watched her unthread a shoelace from his boot and tied his finger to it, making a necklace. Arts and crafts.

When she was done, she looked up at Arthur, most of her suspicion appearing gone and asked in kind, innocent earnest, "want one?" Arthur shook his head. They both climbed back into the van.

The rest of their journey was silent.

CHAPTER TWO

The cold, uncaring glow of fluorescent lights. The chilled, stale oxygen of recycled air. Arthur was home, and it felt good. Home was safe. Home was underground in a reinforced bunker made of concrete and steel. The only enemy down here was inefficiency, a specter as rare as a ghost.

As Arthur marched silently down the concrete corridors of the IRS, he was filled with a sense of hope that was usually punished outside these walls. He was going to be promoted, he was sure of it, and with promotion came the guarantee that he would stay indoors. No longer would he have to risk his life in the harsh United Wastes, sticking his neck out for an audit. No longer would he see another Enforcer like Robert die in the line of duty. No longer would he have to be forced to save children who lacked a childhood. He was free. Free to spend the rest of his life in the confines of a concrete, cubicle jungle.

The black and white checkered linoleum floor beneath him: newly waxed. The bare concrete walls around him: cold and without dust. It was perfection. He walked briskly, doing his best not to dance as he did so, to his shared cubicle. He could not wait to sit, to feel the pleather seat against his back, a seat totally unprepared in design to deal with a human spine. He could not wait to hear the droning clatter of keys being pressed hurriedly as dozens of people typed at the same time. Most of all, he could not wait to gloat, to brag, he could not wait to fly it all into Ralph Siemens' face.

As he turned a corner in the hallway, Arthur was met with a seemingly endless corridor lined with doors on each side. Though the doors were numbered in the dozens, each with their own alphanumeric numbers, they all led to the same room. It was with this design that Arthur could choose any door, including the first one, and find himself in the same large and cluttered space. This, however, was the bureaucracy, the pinnacle of human OCD, and as a breathing bureaucratic prodigy, Arthur had no choice but to walk down the long corridor until he reached the proper door.

He passed a door labeled A13-A14 and he continued forward. He reached door A19-A20 and he gave it no attention. It was not until he was at the very last door, A23-A24 that he stopped. On any normal day, Arthur would not pause outside of this door. He would not consider its steel frame set into a concrete slab. On any normal day, Arthur would simply push the door open. Today, however, was *his* day. Today would be the last day he identified as Auditor #24 and tomorrow there would be a new office drone to fill his pleather seat. Anticipation built inside him, threatening to overtake his calm demeanor with raw joy. With a long, silent breath, Arthur put out his right hand and pushed the door.

The deathly quiet of the hallway was immediately assaulted by a flurry of office noise. Light chatter added to the cacophony of keyboards being pressed madly. A rogue sound of creaking split the air as someone far away adjusted their weight in their seat. He would miss this part of the job, but he wouldn't miss the danger of it. Not all of the cubicles were filled, either because some of the auditors were out in the wasteland, demanding taxes from people like Murder-Man, or because they were deceased from trying to collect taxes from people exactly like Murder-Man. The desks of the dead did not carry tombstones; instead they held a folded over piece of paper, tiny half pyramids with *unassigned* written in a polite and bold font. The regularity of the signs were such that no one in the IRS used that font for anything but death.

There was only one desk ahead of him that was empty, labeled A24. It was his desk, surrounded by a thick wall of concrete, but not completely, to divide it from the other rows. This concrete cubicle was the standard in the doomsday office workplace. Beside his empty spot was a young man just like Arthur, staring contemplatively at his computer screen. His blond hair was parted to the same side as Arthur's, but it came down in a more stringy fashion. He had a face meant for glasses but wore none, and the stubble of his face threatened to become a beard. Also like Arthur, he wore a white collared shirt and a black tie, his slacks neatly pressed and his shoes shined. On his left breast was his work badge with a photograph of him displaying a more clean-cut face. It read Auditor #23, Ralph Siemens, Internal Revenue Services.

There was a healthy competition among the auditors. There was also a decidedly unhealthy competition between most of the auditors. Ralph Siemens was not just a man with an incredibly unfortunate name. No, Ralph was a cheat. Arthur highly suspected that most, if not all of the revenue that Ralph collected was scavenged. He had the same Enforcer for too long. While Arthur dutifully audited citizens of the waste, who were almost always not happy to see him, Ralph likely headed to abandoned buildings to collect what canned food or bullets were left there. He once came back with actual money. No one except IRS employees used actual money. They were twenties but the IRS used two dollar bills almost exclusively. Apparently, no one but Arthur was suspicious. It was an insult. Ralph was an insult - to the job, to the Operations Manual, to everything that the IRS stood for.

Ralph Siemens was a cheat, though he would likely tell you he was a survivalist.

Well, today he would be a loser.

Arthur sat down at his desk and opened his palm. Ralph immediately placed five two dollar bills into it, and said "survived another one I see? I'm getting *real* tired of losing this bet." A plastic smile covered the shared contempt they felt for each other.

"You won't be losing anymore," Arthur announced glibly. Ralph shifted uneasily in his chair.

A short silence fell between the men. Normally, Arthur would get to work at this point. He would boot up his computer and hammer away at its keys. Not today. He turned to Ralph and finally let the smile that had been fighting its way through his professional demeanor shine.

"No!" Ralph said in mock delight. Arthur nodded. "You're finished? You made quota?!"

"Finished my last audit today."

"That's wonderful! Congrats!"

Though the conversation was genial, only one of them was truly happy. Arthur watched as Ralph clenched his hand tighter around his mouse.

"Does this mean...?" Ralph fished.

"Promotion?" said Arthur.

"Yes."

Arthur only smiled in return.

Before either could continue their polite charade, a man walked through their door. He was a studious looking twenty something and was wearing the same office uniform. He marched forward with a clipboard and a mailbag.

"Auditor #A24, Arthur McDowell?" he asked, with a parcel in his hand.

Arthur nodded. The man marked a check on his clipboard and stated: "You have a summons request from the Deputy Commissioner for Operations Support, Henry S. Boyd."

Ralph no longer hid his misery on hearing this, and Arthur's heart skipped a beat. *This is it* he thought, *this is my promotion.*

"Sign here," the man said. Arthur dutifully signed the release form with a flourish.

The man checked the signature, marked another check on his clipboard and tore out a yellow slip, the carbon copy, and handed it to Arthur.

Then he demanded: "Sign here on this release for confirmation that you have received your carbon copy,"

Arthur complied. The man pulled out another carbon copy and handed it to Arthur and then marked a third check on his clipboard. With his job complete the man left abruptly without another word.

Arthur could feel Ralph's hatred beaming at him like a laser. It was absorbed with another smile.

Arthur folded his release receipt neatly, then folded his receipt's receipt, and opened a drawer beneath his desk and carefully filed it. He then took a moment to log the receipt in his drawer's inventory manifest and marked the date and time filed. His work done, he turned to the summons. He was at once stunned by the typeface and centering of the form and fought an urge to measure the negative space on the page. This was no mere memo, this was art. The page stated no more than it had to:

To:: Auditor #A24, Arthur T. McDowell, Below Ground Level 4, Hallway A, Row 23-24, Cubicle #24.

You are summoned to see the Deputy Commissioner for Operations Support, Henry S. Boyd at exactly 2::00 PM Standard Bunker Time.

Henry S. Boyd

The bottom was a dessert he was unprepared for. It was the name signed, *signed!* Arthur now had the autograph of one of the most respected and high ranking officers in the bunker. Bureaucracy could be kind.

Ralph could wait no longer. "That's it then, isn't it? That's the promotion?"

Arthur had no problem drawing this out. "Let's not assume. It could be for anything."

"Don't be an asshole! We both know what that summons means. The Deputy Commissioner for Operations Support, Henry S. Boyd does not bring people to his office for chit-chat. You got it, and we both know it."

"It's going to be an honor to meet him," Arthur said, beaming.

Ralph could not help but put away his loathing at hearing this, and his own fandom took over before being replaced with jealousy. "It will probably be the last time anybody gets to meet him from our division," he said. "He could be promoted to full Commissioner any day now!"

The sentiment was deserved, but Arthur balked at this.

"The Commissioner has held that position since before The War, and he has had it our entire lives, I'm starting to think that he will never die. Boyd won't be promoted anytime soon, you'll get your chance."

Arthur wasn't sure if Ralph deserved this kindness. But it was true, as legendary as Henry S. Boyd was, he could not move upward until the spot was vacant, and the full Commissioner, Jack Dewitt, was never likely to retire.

Henry S. Boyd had done much for the agency. He had led the first census, as well as the more tragic second. He had rewritten protocol, allowing auditors to collect revenue used by the new economy. He was not just a good bureaucrat, he was also a maverick. It would not be going too far to say that once Arthur's father died, Boyd became a role model and hero. It was an honor to meet him, let alone receive the accolades of a promotion from him. Accolades that would promise permanent safety for Arthur.

Accolades that his father never received.

God rest his soul.

Ralph muttered something Arthur did not understand, and then declared "Looks like you'll be my new boss! Congrats, Arthur, Congrats! Good thing I've been your cubicle buddy since the beginning, so it's okay with me if you play favorites!" he smiled.

Oh, I'll play favorites, Arthur thought as he quickly considered sending Ralph to the radioactive craters for an audit. It was something he would never do; send a man to his death, but entertaining the thought was still pleasant.

"It's a shame we won't be making any more bets," Arthur replied.

A shrill, soul-shattering buzz went off in the hallway. It was like broken china making love to a kazoo. It brought pleasure and relief to everyone in a cubicle. It signified one o'clock. Lunchtime.

As if the room were a single organism, every auditor raised and filed themselves in a queue to leave for the bunker's commons area. Only Arthur stayed seated.

"It's SPAM and rice, I'm sure of it," Ralph said confidently as he walked out. Arthur was not surprised by Ralph's eagerness to leave. He never worked anyways. Arthur took a minute to read over his summons once more, and once the rest of his peers were out the door, he followed, elated.

He carried the summons with him.

The queue for lunch began in the hallways and then wound its way down to another level, the fifth of eight levels beneath sea level. The line was like a giant millipede, its starched white abdomen held upright by pressed black pants. Lunch breaks lasted for an hour, and the line, from Arthur's position, took thirty minutes to reach the commons. *I think I'll buy myself a coffee* Arthur thought as he pawed his winnings from Ralph.

There was never a need for change, as all rations were a multiple of two, and all notes were two dollars. The two dollar bill was the pride of the IRS. In the 1970s, when the note was first introduced to lackluster success (Americans simply did not want to use it), the IRS played a long game. Not wanting to pulp or waste the money, the government shrink-wrapped most of the bills being rejected by the citizenry and hid them away in a bunker. The money was to be used to boost the economy once the bombs fell, and as a reserve to pay for whatever the government immediately needed. It was fine that the citizens of the United States in the 1970s refused to use them; the future citizens of the United Wastes would have no choice. Of course, there was no government to be fueled by this money, and now the bills were used internally and as refunds for the poor Wastelander not spry enough to check calories or bullets on their tax return.

Arthur, like the rest of the IRS, received his wage through two dollar bills, but he was also lucky enough to win every bet he made with Ralph. It was with this extra income that Arthur was able to buy the eight dollar coffee ration that he enjoyed on a monthly basis. It was the highest treat and social status marker in the Bureau. His lunch was SPAM and rice.

The common halls were a wide open gash in an otherwise solid slab of concrete. Rows of seemingly endless elongated community tables lined parallel to each other. They were filled with the last of the civil. Once Arthur's meal was paid for, an even ten dollars, he received a small mug of black coffee and a tray with two scoops of rice and a grilled brick of uncut SPAM. Arthur never paid the extra two dollars for gravy. Mindlessly, because everything in the IRS has order, he walked over to his assigned seat and sat down. He did not make eye contact with Ralph.

Arthur's cafeteria row was right next to where the janitors ate, and Arthur was faced towards them. Everybody except the highest pay grade and the ration cooks ate here, and all at the same time. The table he faced was where he grew up, seated next to his father. The table behind him, where the Auditor's supervisors were, is where he will sit next. Arthur was moving on up.

He pulled out his summons, to the great annoyance of Ralph, and read it to himself for the third time. He no longer had to worry about the same fate his father met. He no longer had to repeat the phrase *Guns go up? Don't frown! Fall down!* to himself and pray that no violence met him. More importantly: he could now buy coffee once a week. This was sublime.

As he finished reading his summons, but before he gave in to the imperative of eating his rations, he caught something in the corner of his eye at the janitor's table. It was a breakage in uniform height. The row of janitors grew shorter, and Arthur realized it wasn't some*thing* he saw, it was some*one*. Dressed in a denim jumpsuit too big for her was the little girl, 'Dinner', he had saved that morning, greedily shoveling food into her mouth. Arthur smiled.

The little girl had already been processed through the revenue storage division. Humans may be considered 'calories' in the new economy, but slavery was illegal in the United States, and the IRS was law abiding. The fact that there was no more United States was one that fell on deaf ears to the IRS. She was now an employee of the Internal Revenue Services, and so long as she did not do too good a job, she would never be promoted. She would be safe.

She was young enough that her PTSD would only be debilitating, and not crippling.

Arthur fought off the desire to talk to her, to see if she understood that so long as she did not stand out, she wouldn't become an auditor, that she would be safe if she slacked. He wanted to tell her these things because it was not advice that he took seriously at her age. He wished that he knew then that once he was promoted, he would have to be promoted again to be safe once more. But Arthur was an orderly man, among many in a closed and ordered society; leaving his table was an insult to the carefully planned layout of the commons. Leaving his table was an insult to the IRS.

He hoped that he would someday meet her in the halls as she mopped a floor that never got dirty. He hoped that he could tell her then to skimp on the walls and to keep her head down.

For now, he was happy to see her safe, and that he shared that status.

CHAPTER THREE

Before Arthur could fully enter the office of Deputy Commissioner for Operations Support, Henry S. Boyd, he was urgently pushed aside by a man with a hot mug of coffee. Without a word, this man, who looked like everyone else in the bunker, marched toward the steel desk of the Deputy Commissioner. When he reached the desk, he dutifully picked up an identical but empty mug and replaced it with the mug of coffee he was carrying. In a moment, this man pivoted, marched back toward Arthur and left an initial on a clipboard pinned to the inside of the door. Next, he wrote the date and time and was gone as abruptly as he came. He left behind a stunned Arthur and a distracted-looking Deputy Commissioner. Fifteen seconds of silence reigned supreme before the digital readout above the door read *2::00* exactly. Henry S. Boyd looked up at Arthur from his desk and smiled briefly, "Come in come in!" he said. Arthur obliged and moved into the interior of the office.

Henry S. Boyd's office was meticulous beyond reason. It was a full two feet smaller on each side than the emergency fire exit map that was laminated permanently to the outer hall indicated. This was not a clerical error on the Fire Marshal's part; it only appeared to be smaller because where there should be walls were, in fact, gray steel filing cabinets stacked on top of each other filling every inch from floor to ceiling. There was not a single free millimeter of space between them and the concrete floor and ceiling in which they were contained. If Arthur had not already memorized the fire exit plan from the map and had not seen the dimensions himself, it would be far from a stretch to believe that the walls were the filing cabinets themselves, used as a mad and makeshift bricking substitute.

The only thing that did not appear to be symmetrical in this tomb for files was a single rolling library ladder, which was parked at the back of the office. It occurred to Arthur that had Boyd built this office above ground, any windows that already existed would likely be blocked by the cabinets. It occurred to Arthur that, visually, there would be no difference.

Centered in the the office was Henry S. Boyd himself sitting at his desk. The only blemish in the office was Arthur, still dusty from the audit that morning.

The Deputy Commissioner for Operations Support, Henry S. Boyd, was a tall man, and it was hard for Arthur to imagine he ever needed to use the ladder to reach what he wanted. Aside from being tall, he was an oddity in the United Wastes as he appeared to be in his late fifties. No one grew old in this new cruel world. His high forehead looked like it was designed to hold a couple extra worry lines than the average man was capable of forming. It was topped with greying, thinning hair that looked as if it had never moved a strand in a decade. He sported a broom-like mustache as equally grey as his hair that had done a considerable job at hiding his upper lip. He stared at Arthur, his brow furrowed, bringing his starkly black eyebrows closer than they should ever be allowed to go.

This is a face that could sue a grandfather clock for plagiarism.

Henry S. Boyd broke eye contact first, probably because of boredom more than anything else. As Arthur walked towards the Deputy Commissioner, Mr. Boyd moved a solitary plastic technical ruler from the left side of his desk and measured the distance between his new coffee mug and his computer monitor. As Arthur found himself at rest, a safe but still intimate four feet from the desk, Mr. Boyd then measured the distance between his monitor and where the ruler used to be and placed the ruler back in its position, contented.

"Mr. Arthur T. McDowell, currently assigned as auditor #A24 reporting on time sir," said Arthur, fighting the urge to salute.

The Deputy Commissioner looked back up at Arthur from his ruler, and the faintest of smiles betrayed the cover of his mustache. "So you are, and *currently* indeed. I have summoned you to my humble office in regards to your current position, my boy, but first I have a question for you," he responded, with no muster.

Arthur McDowell's heart sang in anticipation, *I am being promoted*. "Of course sir, anything!" he said. Henry S. Boyd gulped down half of his coffee, measured it back to its proper spot with his ruler, and then did the same for the ruler. Then, with his hands clasped and his elbows on the table, an eyebrow divorced itself from the other and was raised inquisitively. "What is it that we do here, my boy?" he asked, lips still wet from coffee.

The question was deceptive in how unnecessary it was, and Arthur did not understand why it came across as menacing.

"We audit the populace to collect taxes from individuals, as well as businesses and organizations so that the United States Government can run," Arthur stated, and then hurriedly added "sir".

Neither seemed bothered at that moment that there was no government of any kind left that wasn't smoldering in a crater.

"Indeed, indeed," said Boyd. "That is about two-thirds of what we do, but as you are surely aware, we have taken on additional...*duties* since The War. The Revised National Emergency Operations Manual states that the responsibility of census taking is one of our primary duties. Given your shining accolades here with the IRS, I will assume that this lapse of knowledge is a result of a generation gap instead of willful ignorance, as there has not been a census since your childhood. But our duties have been a cycle of census taking, auditing and collecting. This, of course, brings us to your status as an auditor," He downed the other half of his coffee. A few seconds after the mug hit the desk, and was measured once more, a woman with a black tie and black skirt raced into the office with a full mug of coffee. Like the man before her, she replaced the empty mug with the new one and logged herself and the date on the door's clipboard. As quickly as she entered, she was gone, and Arthur found that a heavy dread had replaced his hopeful anticipation. He could only muster a single "Sir?" before Boyd continued his speech.

"It is an unfortunate reality of our job in this great workplace, my boy, but with the census bureau and much of our government lax..." He used 'lax' as a synonym for 'nuclear cinder' "...we have to take up much of the slack. We cannot audit if we do not know where people live, and we don't know where they live unless we find them. And we *must* find them."

"Am, am I not being promoted, sir?" Arthur asked meekly, his fear manifesting in gooseflesh and cold hands.

Another round of measuring the items on Boyd's desk ensued, the silence from him a solid punctuation mark to Arthur's question. He downed half of his coffee and avoided eye contact.

He could guess what was about to happen, and though he had a mouth, he could not bring himself to scream the vulgarities he needed to at this injustice. He should be wailing at the commissioner, demanding that he change his mind He should be throwing cabinets open in impotent protest. Instead, he waited quietly.

Like he was supposed to.

The mug measured once more and everything in its proper place, the Deputy Commissioner broke the silence. "Look, I know how you must feel about this. You are one of our greatest agents, and truth be told, if circumstances were different you would probably have my job someday. You deserve a promotion, and I know how terrible not getting that is." His voice was soft and fatherly. "Mr. McDowell, I have been gunning for full Commissioner my whole life, a position that will not be mine until Commissioner Dewitt steps down or retires. Something he is not likely to do. Like you, I don't make the rules. If it were up to me, tomorrow we would both hold the titles we deserve."

Likely intuiting the tears and protest Arthur was keeping at bay, Boyd continued softly, "I know it's not just the promotion, I know that your father died in the last Great Census. Your file says he was killed by a militia of cannibals?"

Arthur nodded.

Instantly, empathy left the Deputy Commissioner's face and a cold business tone was applied to his voice. "You are being assigned a new Enforcer, by the name of Duke. They have been contracted with us for a full tax season."

Arthur's mind swam with emotions. *What is happening?* repeated like a mad mantra. *No promotion and an Enforcer contracted from the outside? What is happening?* He was not sure which, if any, of the details he should challenge, and so he settled on the last offense "A contracted Enforcer, sir?"

"Yes, it is an unfortunate reality that many of our internal Enforcers have a high mortality rate," Boyd replied. "As of last season we have been contracting outside protection from the United Wastes in the hope to fill their gaps. Enforcer Duke has performed admirably and has been optioned for a permanent position as Enforcer should the census go well. Effective immediately, you are being conscripted as a census taker with the ultimate charge to administer the census in an as of yet unknown territory." The Deputy Commissioner finished the other half of his coffee and fulfilled his measuring ritual while Arthur drowned in desperation.

His dreams of being safe were gone. The last census was one of the most brutal events in the IRS's history. The Revised National Emergency Operations Manual was explicitly clear on the conscripting of an agent. Anyone, no matter their position or current pay grade could be enlisted into census taking if the Deputy Commission of Operations saw it fit. From executive to janitor, any employee of the IRS could be reassigned for essential functions. Census taking was undoubtedly an essential function of the post-war IRS. But in an instant, Henry S. Boyd had not only put Arthur's dreams to death, he had put Arthur to death.

"The IRS needs to expand its reach, Mr. McDowell," Boyd stated. "We have settled on collecting in this single State because our need to survive had to be met first. Now that we are floating in better waters, and now that operations are at their peak since The War, it is our duty to serve the rest of the union. You will be performing a key role in this responsibility. By the end of this meeting, you are to report to Vehicle Bay 13 to collect a van for your journey, the assigned rations, and your new Enforcer. By the end of the day I expect you to be on your way outside of our known territory and into one of the adjacent states. The details of the area for your census are being shipped to Vehicle Bay 13 as we speak."

Boyd looked at his coffee. "Upon completion of the census you will return with the supervising position you so deserve. I am sorry, Arthur. This is only a detour in your career, but all detours lead back to your rightful destination."

Arthur wanted to shout, Arthur should shout, but his sense of duty prevented him.

Mr. Boyd continued: "Personally, I do not expect this to be like last time. We are only being thorough, but the area should be nearly empty. I would not expect anything more dangerous than you have already experienced. If you were any other agent I would be worried, but there should be no more than a few scattered families, at worst a tribe. Raider country is in the opposite direction."

Arthur felt some relief. Not a lot, but enough to quiet his most dire of fears.

The door opened and a man with red hair holding a replacement mug of coffee rushed in, almost spilling it. He gathered the old mug, and before he could pivot, the Deputy Commissioner yelled "You're late!" and stamped the word 'infraction' on a pink slip from his desk. The man looked sullenly at the floor, took the pink slip from the Deputy Commissioner and filled out his name and time on the door.

Before the red-haired man left, he said in a shaky voice, "It won't happen again, sir."

"I know, "the Deputy Commissioner whispered, and the red-haired man left.

Ruler to mug, ruler to an empty spot, and then mug to mouth. Henry S. Boyd drank greedily. It was the most coffee Arthur had ever seen someone consume.

"Honestly, this is good news," Mr. Boyd reported to Arthur. "With this census, our operation may expand and, when completed, you will find yourself supervising a new generation of Auditors to the new region! Think of yourself as a pioneer to a new world, my boy. I wouldn't trust this mission to just anybody. You are the most competent Auditor I have seen in years, and once this is done I am sure you will be a competent supervisor!"

Arthur was conflicted in his emotions. Boyd was giving him praise, and a promise for the very job that would help him grow old, but for now he had to work with an outsider on a job that had doomed his father. It was hard to tell how much of this was genuine disdain at his circumstances, and how much was hurt pride. The Deputy Commissioner himself had said that this should not be dangerous. After all, census taking was just filling out a questionnaire; it was not nearly as intense as auditing. He wouldn't be threatening to take from the desperate, only counting the needy. Yes, this was unexpected, but wasn't it an honor to serve the IRS? Wouldn't a last foray into a sparsely populated wasteland to herald a new era in tax collection only cement his legacy and help him move upward from supervisor?

Arthur McDowell looked into the eyes of the Deputy Commissioner whose warm smile now betrayed the cover of his grey mustache once more. "I trust only the best for this mission," he said.

Only the best. This flattery had done it for Arthur. This wasn't what he had wanted, but his hero, the personification of bureaucracy, of civility in a cruel wasteland, had just referred to him as 'the best'. He had to live up to that. He couldn't disappoint the Deputy Commissioner. The fact was that no matter how he felt about it, Arthur had no choice but to do his job. But he could now do it with a little pride. It was a bitter pride, but pride nonetheless.

"You can count on me sir," Arthur reported with half reluctant gusto.

Henry S. Boyd looked down at his desk. "Good," he said, as he signed a white slip of paper, confirming their meeting, and handed it to Arthur for his signature. Arthur clicked his pen and signed his name with a flourish. Seconds later, the Deputy Commissioner peeled out the yellow carbon copy and handed him it.

His second autograph of the day.

"You should find Enforcer Duke waiting for you in Vehicle Bay 13," said Boyd. "The Van Master should have you pumped and ready. Godspeed and good luck, my boy, this time in four days I hope to see you here at my desk again, as a Supervisor to Auditors #A1-#A24."

This would put him in charge of Ralph, and would ensure his safety.

"Thank you, sir," was all Arthur could manage.

His career was stalled, but only temporarily, and for a cause that he believed in. It was hard for him to think that just moments ago he had felt so deflated, and had believed that certain doom was ahead of him.

As Arthur walked out of Henry S. Boyd's office he was met with the tearful sobs of the red-haired man who dared to be late in the Deputy Commissioner's scheduled consumption of coffee. The man was shaking, the pink slip crumpled. Arthur gave him no regard as he left and made the trek back to his desk before heading out to the Vehicle Bay. He was too consumed with his own thoughts to notice that the man with red hair trailed closely behind. Any time Arthur was confronted with disappointment, any time that terrible dread at his new dire chore threatened to surface, he would repeat those three magic words in his head: *only the best*.

CHAPTER FOUR

There are three rules of the road. They aren't particularly hard to remember, nor are they mired in wit. To women like Rabia, they were taught at a young age instead of nursery rhymes. They were taught alongside the Ten Commandments. But the rules of the road had more utility, and they had brevity on their side.

Rule number one: do not drive at night.

Of course, knowing your lessons and learning your lessons are two different things.

Rabia Duke, consummate professional and former Sheriff of one of the largest United Wastes caravans, she learned this lesson early. While Arthur was mopping the floors of the IRS bunker, Rabia rode in a modified big rig with her mother. The truck, which was as much a home as it was transportation, was the only privilege she had growing up. Considering that she was a black girl in the American wasteland, any kind of privilege was held onto with grit and desperation. The United States was a cruel, racist, and misogynistic place *before* the bombs fell. By the time Rabia was riding shotgun in a truck covered in sheet metal armor counting bullets for her mother, the United Wastes had become a cruel, racist, and misogynistic playground. She was already the least important type of person in America, and that was before she knew that she liked women as much as she liked men.

Most first-generation wasters were illiterate, so Rabia's mother saw to it that her daughter would not be among them. Their caravan, like many other collectives in the post-apocalypse, was run by a 'Shepherd' who had more in common with cult leaders than he did priests. It was important to Rabia's mother that Rabia was able to interpret the bible for herself, instead of relying on the feverish spit that came out of the Shepherd's mouth. This, it would turn out, would be her mother's greatest mistake.

At the age of eleven, when she would learn her first lesson of the road, Rabia Duke discovered the book *Hell's Angels*. The long hours on the road were boring and she'd found the ill-gotten book while she and her mother scavenged for canned food among the rubble of man. It was the only non-fiction book she had ever read that resembled the world around her. She was taught to wield a gun for hunting and protection. She was taught to wield the written word to obey the will of God. But instead, she played with the words of Thompson and Bukowski, and she played with the safety off.

Dr. Thompson was her favorite. He seemed like a perfectly rational and tempered person compared to the savages that roamed the roads. This little girl, her only toys a mixed bag of crayons and a Geiger Counter, related to a Gonzo journalist better than any of God's chosen people. Hell, they even had the same surname half of the time Thompson did something terribly illegal.

It was *Hell's Angels* that she was reading when her mother told her to lock her doors. Some of the men were drinking. Stupid with liquor and emboldened by the full moon, they had decided that it was a perfect time for motorcycle jousting. Rabia protested. Motorcycle jousting was her favorite spectator pastime, why should she miss it just because it was dark out? Her mother told her to watch the horizon.

The sound of motorcycle engines had nothing to compete with during the night, their headlights like miniature suns piercing the darkness. The men had unwittingly announced their presence to predators.

The raiders came with all of Thompson's madness, and all of Old Testament God's fury and cruelty. The consequences of breaking the road's first rule were on full display. It was as if the Hell's Angels had come screaming out of the pages of her book to bring the second apocalypse to the world. Her mother kept her still and quiet. They hid behind the front seats in total darkness. Rabia's mother could cover her daughter's mouth to keep her from crying, but she could not also cover her ears to protect her from the screaming.

The Raiders only tried to get into the heavily armored rig twice, once with brute force, and once with a Molotov cocktail. Neither worked. Rabia survived her first lesson that night without sleep or hope.

Rule number two: you scavenge for yourself.

This was a rule that her mother broke often. It was a simple calculus with no room for empathy. What you found was yours unless you wanted to starve. Like most children of the United Wastes, Rabia learned to scavenge the moment she could walk without falling. It should have been then that her mother stopped providing for her.

When Rabia found no food for herself, but still ate from her mother's bounty, she needed only to see the anguished face of her starving mother. This lesson needed no grand slaughter to make itself clear. Care for others and you will suffer.

Yet the lesson repeated every now and then. Rain fell like murky spit on the irradiated dust the day she got her first period. This, according to her mother, was lucky. It gave them an excuse to hide inside the rig. The men had begun to notice her. Her pants were ruined and the stain was something that the Shepherd would want to talk about. The Shepherd was always looking for another sister wife. While the hateful rain turned dust into mud, Rabia's mother scavenged for tampons and replacement clothing. Rabia hid in the rig, confused, ashamed, and frightened. Her mother instructed her to read Leviticus, but instead she read *Generation of Swine*. Her childhood had never properly begun in the United Wastes, but now it looked as though it had come to an abrupt end.

Lesson Two was not just a survival calculus. No. Lesson Two was also practical. Her mother came back with tampons, sure, that was not a problem. But she also came back with a dress. Rabia hated dressing girly. That day, Rabia learned that if you want to dress yourself, you scavenge for yourself.

She grew, but she stayed short. While her mother towered above some of the men at six feet, Rabia peaked at five five. She grew in other places though, and her mother told her that she was beautiful. The men said things that would make even Dr Thompson feel violated. Wearing a dress was a bad idea. It was the last nice thing that Rabia let her mother do for her. Well, that was until she met Melody...

Lesson Three: Never trade with slavers. Even though it shouldn't have been, this one was hard learned. Blue eyes and warm smiles can affect a girl's judgment. Rabia didn't like to dress girly, but, well, she liked it when others did, and Melody? Melody wore dresses better than she ever could.

Rabia's mother had been dead two years since that lesson. Rabia had learned to fight better than most men and was quicker to pull the trigger too. Her mother did her best to raise her well, despite the challenges of the United Wastes. She did her best to impart the important lessons. Rabia ignored the ancient texts of Luke and John, and drank, smoked, and cursed better than the men she killed. She liked her girls as much as she liked her boys, assuming that the boys weren't bleeding psychopaths. There was much about her that disappointed her mother.

Her mother would have preferred a different type of daughter. But at least she imparted the three rules of the road to her before she died. Those rules were now deeply instilled.

CHAPTER FIVE

Arthur's new Enforcer looked like someone who was suspiciously not the best for the job. Oh, she looked like she could handle herself in a fight, so that would not be a problem and, based on her worn, custom gear, it looked like she was definitely not someone to fuck with. But what set off Arthur's internal alarms was the copious amount of cursing and yelling she was doing at the Van Master, along with the two cigarettes she was smoking simultaneously - in a no smoking zone. It was hard to tell from the other side of the van bay, but one of the cigarettes looked like it was filled with something other than tobacco.

Almost silently, Arthur began to cross the bay. The Van Master was cowering at the flying spittle from the Enforcer's yelling. Arthur could not hear what the mouse-like Van Master had just said, but his Enforcer's words were loud and clear.

"You Goddamn swine! You hear me you unconscionable bastard?! Those supplies are necessary, *necessary* for the very survival of our mission! YOU HAVE DOOMED US YOU HATEFUL PIG BASTARD!" The Van Master looked helplessly around him, hiding his head behind a clipboard at the abuse being volleyed at him.

Her voice carried and echoed well in Bay 13. It was a cavernous-like enclosure, an area that was likely older than the bunker. This was the underground parking level of the old IRS building, and a generation after the building was mostly leveled it was still full of vehicles. The exception was that the parking lot was now used as a repair shop instead of for parking. There were about a dozen white minivans on this floor, all of them identical to the one leased to Arthur earlier that day, lined up in an orderly fashion. Work should have been done on a few of them now, but the mechanics had paused, all of them looking curiously at the scene Arthur's Enforcer was making.

The Van Master clocked Arthur and beckoned him over with a desperate tone, "Are you Arthur McDowell, Census Taker #A24?"

Arthur winced at his new title. "Yes, that's me," he answered, "What seems to be the problem?" The Enforcer grabbed Arthur's hand, her grip cold and firm. With eye contact, she shook his hand enthusiastically. Her demeanor was as cool now as it was hot just seconds ago. If Arthur hadn't seen it he would not have thought her capable of such white-hot rage.

"Rabia, Rabia Duke, Enforcer," she said. "It's good to see a man who looks reasonable in this godforsaken hellscape." Even *godforsaken hellscape* was said at a level that sounded rational, nothing like the cursing a moment ago.

Rabia released Arthur's hand and lay back against a white van. Her dark brown skin appeared darker than it was in the poor light and, despite the darkness in Bay 13, aviator sunglasses covered her eyes. Her militant clothing was worn and old, likely scavenged, her shorts doing nothing to hide the many scars covering her legs.

Rabia Duke smelled permanently of cigarettes and dust, but the acrid smell of tobacco was stronger due to her lips holding both a cigarette and something else like a cigarette, both in one corner of her mouth. Her thick and kinky hair was stuffed under a military cap, the word PROFESSIONAL written on it in permanent marker. A shotgun, which was almost bigger than her frame was held securely behind her with a strap over her shoulders. It was the only weapon that Arthur could see, though he suspected she had more hidden in her many pockets. It was spray-painted red with the phrase 'Fly Swatter' etched chaotically along its barrel in long scratches.

Though Arthur was a full three inches taller than Rabia, he got the sense that she was looking down at him. He would probably find her attractive if she wasn't so intimidating.

"This weird Nazi car-salesman here wants us dead. He can't be reasoned with, I tried," said Rabia through the two smokes in her mouth.

"She wants some unorthodox equipment that we cannot provide," the Van Master pleaded.

Rabia prodded her finger at the Van Master's chest accusingly. "Unorthodox?" she said. "We are going into unknown territory, you geek! You can't tell us what's unorthodox if you can't tell us what we'll find out there. Good God, man! Have some sympathy for the damned." At that, she drew in a heavy amount of smoke, crossed her arms, and looked away. "These are bad omens on the horizon, cowboy," she said, to no one in particular.

Work in the garage started up again, albeit a bit reluctantly. Eyes still leered at the trio from suspicious corners, but otherwise, Bay 13 was back to its usual heartbeat. The Van Master handed Arthur a clipboard. "This is the manifest for your journey that was obtained from the Deputy Commissioner of Operations' desk. You are to receive a week's worth of water for two, a week's worth of canned rations and dry rations, mostly spam and instant mashed potatoes, a water recycling kit, two shovels, and camping gear. It says nothing about drugs, sir."

Rabia Duke launched herself off of the van and towards the Van Master, her finger at his chest and her face only a couple inches from his. "You rat bastard! How is a professional supposed to do her job without rum? Without whiskey? Most of what I gave you was a wish list, sure, I can supply my own screamers. And if you don't have the pound of grass in those giant stores of yours, that's fine. Hell, I don't even trust you to know the difference between a psilocybin and a shiitake mushroom, but goddammit man, a professional needs that alcohol!"

The Van Master took a step back, but Rabia quickly closed the gap and pushed her finger into his chest as hard as she could. "AND WE'LL NEED THOSE GRAPEFRUITS FOR THE SCURVY!"

"I-I told you, ma'am, you can buy that alcohol at our wares store if need be, but—"

"Buy? BUY THEM?! I'm a patriot, you swine! These things should come stocked in that Goddamn minivan! There is no way I can afford your wares anyways. You selfish bastards hike up your prices too high for anyone without an 'employee discount' and despite the fact that I have been contracted—"

"*Contracted* ma'am," the Van Master interjected, "the employee discount is for salaried workers only."

This is why we shouldn't hire outsiders Arthur thought. *No respect for the rules.* He had no want for any further confrontation, and if he was to work with this 'professional' and survive, it was better that they leave the bay on good terms. He offered his hand up between the two in peace, "I have an employee discount, Miss Duke," he said. "If it is that important—"

"It is a necessity," she corrected.

"If it is a necessity then you can pay me back, and we can be on our way," Arthur replied, calmly.

"You see that, you weird Nazi scum?" Rabia spat at the Van Master, smoke billowing out of her mouth. "*That* is what a reasonable, God fearing man looks like!" She jerked the clipboard out of Arthur's hand and signed the manifest furiously, not waiting to receive her carbon copy. Arthur picked the copy up off of the floor.

She patted Arthur on the back. "Come on now, let me let you buy a girl a drink," she said, almost flirtatiously.

All eyes of the garage were on them, their suspicion piercing. Only Arthur seemed to mind their judgmental gaze, as Rabia's walk became brisk, even graceful. He followed behind her, self-conscious. No one shouted in the IRS. This was a place for civility and order, a sanctuary from the heart of darkness that reigned supreme on the outside. Yet, here was an outsider, brought in from necessity, bred in the United Wastes and raised by its callous, cruel hand. What understanding did she have of Arthur's world?

He had worked with plenty of other Enforcers, and though they were a different breed from the office drones, they sure as hell weren't as mercurial as Rabia. They, like Arthur, were mostly raised in the cold and safe halls of tax central. It clearly didn't bother Rabia that their peers were looking disdainfully at them, but that's what bothered Arthur most of all. What would they think of him, associating with her, even buying what she wanted? What if they had heard he was up for a promotion, but instead was back on the road with that animal? What sort of rumors would be forged in that vacuum of information? What sort of falsities would they imagine to justify his fall from grace? It was maddening to think about.

You'll have to spend a week with her his mind volunteered as chills and gooseflesh spread across his body.

"I appreciated your assistance there," Rabia said, happily. "I'm sure with a little more abuse that coward would have bent, but you never can be too sure of the iron will of bureaucrats. They are not imaginative; if it doesn't add up on their forms, it just isn't possible."

"I'm a bureaucrat," Arthur replied with a mixture of pride and annoyance.

"I know that, but so far you are willing to buy a professional necessary supplies and a girl a drink, so you are forgiven," Rabia said with jest.

"My last Enforcers didn't need to drink," Arthur replied coldly.

"What of it? Huh? Did them a lot of good. All of them dead."

"They died in the line of duty."

"Bullshit," said Rabia. "They died while you laid on your back trying to rob desperate people. I've been around to see this madness, been on the other side of it too. There is nothing honorable about what we do."

Arthur stopped. *Who does this woman think she is?* he thought, not daring to say it and end this short-lived peace.

"We don't rob people," he said. "We simply remind them of their civic duty—"

"Civic duty?" Rabia interrupted. "My God, man, what civilization do you see out there? Listen, the difference between us and your average raider camp is that the raiders don't have the sense to leave their victims behind. It's a brilliant racket we got here - take enough to make us rich but leave them alive and with enough supplies to get more the next time we come back. It's a winning idea in the United Wastes, I'll give you that, but let's call it what is. Without a social contract to sign, we are thieves with an ideology."

"I've heard you have been with us for some time," Arthur said to Rabia's back. "What happened to your other Auditor?"

Rabia turned her head to answer but continued forward without missing a step. Smoke covered the parts of her face that her sunglasses didn't hide. "The same thing that happened to your Enforcers. As your new Enforcer, I recommend you stay on my good side."

Arthur did what he had been doing his entire life. He followed. Begrudgingly, which is the first time he had that feeling while doing what he was told, but he followed still. *Only the best* he repeated in his mind, but this time it was far from comforting. It wasn't uncommon for an Enforcer to fail at keeping their Auditor alive. It happened. Yet there was nothing comforting in Rabia, nothing there to calm his fear of dying. The others had been true believers, doing their job for a civil future. In the short time he had talked with her, it was hard to say if Rabia believed in anything. He had a strange feeling that this conviction in believing in nothing meant that she would even balk at nihilism for being too idealistic.

The two, neither happy for the other's company, reached the closest thing the United Wastes had to a convenience store: The IRS Wares Store. In its lowest sub level, the IRS bunker kept the cache of taxes it had collected, along with the massive amount of shrink-wrapped two dollar bills. It was the largest horde in the United Wastes and was by far the most unique. Once the IRS officially recognized the barter system that much of the United Wastes had been using, the store filled with everything from toilet paper to weapons. These wares stores served as a 'currency exchange' for the agents, allowing them to turn in their two dollar bills for anything their hearts desired. The one on this floor had taken up the space of six parking spaces, with scavenged wood and steel used to partition its goods from the rest of the garage with an orderly wall. Food, feminine hygiene, bullets, and even reading material filled scavenged bookcases wall to wall. All of it guaranteed to be free from radiation.

It was a tiny oasis of plenty in a world without water.

Rabia looked within, lustfully.

After seeing Rabia, and intuiting her order, the clerk, a balding man who had never been outside of the bunker's walls, turned his back on them and gathered supplies. He returned with a quart of tequila, a quart of rum, two handles of Wild Turkey 101 bourbon, three cans of grapefruit and a carton of smokes. All of it was older than Arthur and Rabia.

"You are going to have to be less particular of your bourbon, Miss Duke, we are going to run out of it at some point. There is no one left making it," the clerk said with a wry smile.

"There's still the irradiated stuff," she replied. "And if you think for a moment that it is any more dangerous than the stuff that isn't irradiated then you clearly have never had a drop of Wild Turkey yourself."

A small cloud of smoke caught beneath the brim of her hat. The clerk's smile faded, and a deft hand punched a calculator at the counter.

"That will be two hundred dollars or an equal amount of calories and bullets," the clerk stated, without looking up.

Rabia jabbed Arthur with her elbow, ushering him to fix the situation. Reluctantly, he moved forward.

"It is my buy today," Arthur said. The clerk looked up with muted surprise.

"As a non-outsider, the face value exchange will be one hundred dollars," the clerk stated, without checking his calculator.

Arthur counted out fifty bills and, as he handed them over, Rabia slapped him on the back affectionately. "You're a good man, Charlie Brown," she said.

"Who's Charlie Brown?" Arthur asked, confused.

"No idea, it was something my mother used to say. I think he was a kid who went bald from chemotherapy, back when radiation was good. Anyway, let's get a move on," Rabia said, walking away, leaving Arthur to carry everything. He quickly grabbed the heavy load in a half panic after realizing that he was going to be left behind.

This wasn't fair. They should be counting their inventory, meticulously checking that everything was in its place. This wasn't just because he was orderly, to the point that it was nearly debilitating at times, but because their survival depended on it. They should be on their way to their destination, scouting for a safe camping site. Traveling at night in a vehicle was too dangerous, it made too much noise and the headlights would be like flares leading the cruel to them. Instead, they were buying drugs.

Somehow, Arthur had lost control of the situation, and he was supposed to be in charge.

He should have been barking orders, but instead, he buried his anger. He would straighten things up on the road, where there was no one to judge him for his outburst.

Rabia Duke was the first to their van. After a pause, she slid open the side door with the pomp of a magician, revealing the rations and gear leased to them. Yet that was not all that was there. A gun case of every size filled much of the van's floor, each one of them labeled ESCALATION on strips of duct tape. The only cases without this label instead read TOOLS and MEDICINE. The latter dwarfed the toolbox. Rabia kicked its latches open.

"I suppose you want to count everything," she mumbled, holding up a hand, gesturing for the liquor. Arthur complied and watched as she stuffed the drinks into the case. Then he saw it: a plethora of drugs old and new. None of them were for illness.

"What is that?" Arthur accused.

"Aside from the guns and a few pipe bombs," Rabia replied, "we have multi-colored uppers, downers, screamers, laughers, and some bits of an unknown purple crystal I jacked from a raider, which I haven't dared to try yet. I don't actually know if you're supposed to smoke it, but judging by his bulging eyes before I killed him I would say it is a safe bet that's what he did with it. There's also some high powered Shaman's Milk in there, I'm sure the curdling doesn't matter. Some pre-war pellets of MDMA and LSD, both pure, I've tested them, some ayahuasca, a six-pack of only the darkest beer, and a brown bottle I found on a dead woman labeled 'no'."

Before Arthur could protest, and before he could point out that it was all federally illegal (something that apparently mattered), Rabia kicked the latches back down and looked at Arthur with intense regard. Her sunglasses were now slightly down, revealing her brown eyes, Arthur couldn't decide if it was their beauty that was seducing him or their desperate craving for madness that they broadcast. A Cheshire cat grin spread from ear to ear, her cigarette and funny smelling hand-roll still clenched between teeth.

"This is going to be a wild ride," she said.

CHAPTER SIX

Rabia Duke drove as if she was a kamikaze screaming towards a cliff, yet her demeanor was mostly calm. She kept a vigilant eye on the horizon, which looked murky. This was common in the United Wastes and was nothing to worry about. Not much had been said since they had left the safe confines of the bunker, and she could not yet say if this was because Arthur was not happy to be near her. There was an equal possibility that no words could be heard above the blaring Rock 'n' Roll cassette tape playing over the van's speakers, something labeled *The Doors* that Rabia had been playing nonstop.

This of course was a rational excuse for why he had been silent, but very few words had been exchanged the night before. After setting up camp, and eating separately, she had eaten something from her MEDICINE bag and had taken a bottle of tequila to her burlap tent. She had briefly shaken the bottle at Arthur with kind eyes and said "Want?", but when Arthur shook his head, there was nothing said until morning. Arthur had spent the night alone in his tent, presumably re-reading the old pre-war map given to them, his area of census measured out in a red ink border. She was disappointed by his distance, but also disappointed that the something from her bag had done very little.

She suspected that Arthur would be entirely content if this lack of communication lasted for the rest of their journey. His trust was probably hard earned, but she could hardly fault him for that. She was the same way. Besides, he had probably never met a woman as kickass as her. Men tend to get pouty when they are around kickass women.

Rabia, however, no matter how callous or mercurial, was more amicable for socialization. She regarded Arthur with the corners of her eyes as she drove, noting that he was wearing a seatbelt, even though there was no more law requiring him to do so. There was no seatbelt around her, and in truth if she was the van's only occupant there wouldn't be any pants either. After a moment of staring at him she turned the volume down and Arthur sat up straight. "What is it? Did you hear something?!" he asked with frightful urgency.

She hadn't noticed before, but Arthur was incredibly tense. His knuckles were white and sharp from his bones, mirroring the pinhole like irises bulging out of his sockets in cold fear. The awkward silence between them was likely this sense of terror eating at his psyche. They had little in common, but Arthur struck Rabia as a people pleaser, so surely those differences would have melted for this man's need for social equilibrium. She was willing to bet on it, and she only bet on sure things. This poor bastard had probably been stressing himself out since they left the safety of the bureaucratic snipers posted throughout the urban wastes. Though Rabia's job was to keep him safe, and not to make him *feel* safe, she supposed that she could do the man a kindness and put the sweating bastard at ease.

"No, nothing aside from the gypsy ramblings from the speakers," she replied. "We are in the dust plains now, there won't be any land pirates for miles. The only thing we need to look out for is the squealing of our Geiger Counter. Just wanted to have a professional conversation. I know that it's easy to get off on the wrong foot with me, but I promise you I am one of the good guys. You doing okay?" Rabia said all this as sweetly as she was capable, which was at the very least slightly more sugary than a saltine.

Arthur did not answer her immediately, and with the Rock 'n' Roll no longer screeching like a banshee the only noise that could be heard was the labored purr of the engines and the faint blast of sand from the outside.

The dust plains were vast, a picture of infertile sand spanning in every direction. This was once farm country, the heart and soul of America. Corn and wheat once shot up from the ground like harpoons out of a cannon; there was so much of the stuff growing so quickly that only a mechanized nation could even attempt containing it. Now, the only grain that came from this country was of a fine rock, whittled down by wind. Rumor on the caravan said that the whitest grains were the remnants of bone, blown away from the equally deserted city that the dust plains surrounded.

Arthur sighed deeply, and had begun to relax. Rabia was right, he was far too polite to simply ignore her, and so she would have the conversation she wanted. She would never admit it aloud, but she did relish the chance to talk to a civil man. It was a nice change of pace from your common waste-lander who was only interested in getting into her pants from conniving or by force.

Arthur's mouth opened to say something, but then closed quickly. He stirred in his seat, shifting his weight awkwardly. "Yeah, I'm okay," he said, "just shaken. The unknown scares me, and I've never been this far from the bunker. I never realized how comforting the IRS border snipers were until today. The furthest away from the bunker I have ever been is just outside the suburbs, and they're only a day's walk from the bunker and only hours from the safety of the snipers."

"Indeed," Rabia responded, letting the wheel go to light a cigarette. She made no effort to slow down, but kept an eye on the murky horizon.

It took just a few seconds for Arthur to realize that he had only answered her question and had not regarded the rest of her statement. "The IRS wouldn't hire you if you were a bad guy, I suppose. I don't know; I'm just not used to outsiders." More sand blasted the windshield. The mechanical purr of the engines raged on. Arthur found the need to clarify. "Not that there is anything wrong with outsiders..."

The Geiger counter squeaked as quietly as a tamed hamster.

"Holy magnet of destitution!" Rabia cursed as she slammed on the breaks. Arthur's seatbelt tightened and dug firmly into his chest.

Rabia looked down and over her shades, her eyes as bulged as Arthur's just moments ago. Panic rang in her head. The horizon. "Shelter!" she hissed. "My God, man, we need shelter! Do you see that god damn storm brewing?"

Had her eyes not been trained to see it, had she not spent an entire childhood staring off into the distance fearing this very boogeyman, they could have driven into the worst of it. The Geiger Counter chirped once more.

A dust storm.

"What? What's wrong?" Arthur asked, gasping for breath.

"That brown haze in the distance. It's picking up momentum. This van isn't lined with lead, is it?"

Arthur shook his head. "With the scarcity of gas and the rapid increase in its price in the economy, the IRS elected to go without lead plating in our vans to save on weight. It has saved the agency—"

"Black hearted bastards! We need to find the van cover

before this thing picks up some mojo and we get cooked alive in this vicious can!"

They were a day's drive from the city, and structures like barns or farm houses that used to be out in the plains had been sheared away from the earth by the hot, irradiated dust storms that Rabia now feared were ahead of them.

"Wha—" was all Arthur could manage.

"You see that haze out there?" Rabia asked, deciding not to illicit patience. "That haze is probably six hours out, but covers the entire horizon. Those winds blow about as fast as this van goes and they blow with irradiated dust. When that foul thing hits, it will be like a sand blaster having sex with a microwave. One of those things is inconvenient, *both* is nuclear castration!"

"Wha—"

"THERE IS NO TIME TO BE VERBOSE! Chug half of your canteen then grab one of the shovels. We are going to dig hatefully, then tip this bastard van on its side and into our hole, and we camp out here until that storm passes or God blinks and forgets we're here!"

"Umm."

"NOW, DAMMIT!

Rabia leapt from the van, threw the side door open and pawed desperately at their supplies. Arthur was frozen until the urgency finally sunk in. Knowing that their lives depended on his quick action, he unbuckled his seat belt, opened the glove box, and subtracted one full canteen from the inventory list.

"I said NOW!" Rabia screamed from outside.

She said dig hatefully, so hatefully they dug. The Geiger Counter chirped softly with long pauses between each piece of song, but as the hole grew deeper, and the storm closer, the chirps became more elongated and more frequent.

They paused only for water, and only for as long as Rabia let them. Her murderous gaze stopped Arthur from subtracting from the manifest (which was fine, because Arthur had a knack for keeping these things in his head anyway). Rabia was fit, having spent her life fighting off death, but her frame was slender, and not accustomed to the terrible labor. But she was still quicker at digging than Arthur.

It was not that Arthur lacked the work ethic, and although he was a little taller than Rabia, and a little broader, the only labor his body had known was running in fright. This made him terrible at digging.

The day's light had muted, but not from the sun's march forward, but because the storm that once looked like a small haze in the horizon had closed its distance and was now like a mountain, fluid in movement. Hours had gone by. They dug down, then they dug in. Both had become exhausted long ago. They kept digging.

More hours. More digging.

The hole had to be taller than the van. The wind had to blow over it not into it. Rabia sliced at the ground with her shovel, and Arthur did the same.

Their hole was dug.

There was now a deep wedge in the dust plain.

． ． ．

After Rabia had moved the van closer to the hole, and parallel to its wide berth, she grabbed a jack from the repair kit and moved it upwards from its side as high as it would go. The pair spent what little strength they had left ramming their bodies against the van in quick succession. After their fourth wave, it tipped over and into the hole.

Within a few minutes, they were inside, seated on the walls with their backs against the floor. Rabia wasted no time in getting into the liquor. "Want?" she asked, sweetly. Arthur shook his head, and started subtracting from the manifest. "That storm will be over our heads soon," Rabia continued, "we stay in here until that Geiger Counter is as quiet as a grave." She took a swig of rum, relieved to feel it burn her throat.

"This will hold us up a day," Arthur said, glumly. It was a strange sentiment to hear aloud, and Rabia chuckled woefully at it.

"That is the least of our worries G-Man," she said. "But don't worry, once this clears I'll get you there so you can count your heads.

"How did you learn to do that?" Arthur asked, kindly, the first time his voice sounded sincere in wanting to learn about her. *Nothing cracks nuts like a ball breaking hellstorm,* Rabia thought to herself, glad to finally be speaking on friendly terms.

"I was born into one of the great caravans," she replied. "A large tribe of civilians carrying and scavenging anything they can get their hands on to whatever settlement was willing to trade. My mother kept me on watch on top of her semi-truck's cab." Rabia wiped sweat from her face. She paused to take another swig, the sickly sweet taste of the rum washed out whatever dust was left in her mouth.

"She kept me up there to look out for things like the hell-beast about to be on top of us now, as well as land pirates, raiders and slavers. She trained my eyes for all of these things, but mostly I think she kept me up there because it meant I was out of reach from lustful men. While you were likely learning bureaucratic dogma and why anything but blue and black ink is a sin, I was learning the language of the dead planet we are stuck on."

She did not mean this last part bitterly, but could tell that Arthur picked up on the implication that he was privileged. Before he could say anything, a sound not unlike an avalanche blasted above. The howling fury of the dust storm engulfed their small enclosure. The Geiger Counter clicked off excitedly, and Rabia continued on.

"We had to do this sort of thing often when coming through the dust plains. It is normally no problem anywhere else as there is always a derelict structure to hide under. But out here there is only down for shelter. Don't worry about the noise; it is only as bad as it sounds."

What little light there had been in the overturned van was mostly extinguished. A silent moment passed before either of their eyes had a chance to adjust. The only light source was the burning cherry tip from Rabia's newly lit cigarette. Arthur was close enough that Rabia could feel the warmth from his body. If Arthur didn't enjoy this, then he was too tired to move. Rabia took a swig nervously.

"Give the devil her due when it is deserved," Rabia said. "Only an outsider could have saved you here."

By the expression wrote on his face, Rabia could tell Arthur wanted to rebuke this, but he decided against it and relented.

"I'm just glad I don't have to file a 21B Radiation Sickness form," he said. "The margin on the tables is too wide."

With a lull in the conversation threatening to turn into a

full and awkward silence, Rabia changed the topic after exhaling on her cigarette.

"You have a reputation among the other Enforcers," she said, cleaning her sunglasses with her shirt. "The fact that you have outlived four of them is both incredible and concerning."

"I don't try to get them killed if you are thinking—"

"Not at all, it is as ugly as a whore's knee-sock out there. People die. The other Enforcers are less suspicious about that than you think. Believe me, if I thought you were a back stabber, I wouldn't have taken the job. The reputation is a good one, if not a little baffling."

"Oh?"

"They say that you always bring them back, the dead Enforcers. You always carry their bodies back with you. Why is that?"

Arthur replied with a staggered noise that was not exactly a word. There was another lull, and it definitely became an awkwardness

"It's not something we do in the caravans," Rabia said, breaking the silence. "When someone dies, they are dead weight, so it's important to your survival to leave them where they lay. If you catch someone dragging a corpse, it's because they plan on eating it and not share."

She was answered with the howling blast of sand above them, and for a moment believed that this was the only answer she was going to get. Arthur let out a long lungful of air, and then he broke his silence.

"There is no dignity anymore," he said. No one has it. I don't think it's anyone's fault, given the circumstances, but people deserve to have it. I bring them back so that they can be buried, and so that their families can get whatever peace they can from it. I know that that's next to none, but it's always worth the try." Burying the dead was a foreign idea to

Rabia in practice. People died. But she had heard her mother speaking about the old ways from time to time. Arthur respected the dead. He did what no one asked him to do, and he did it because it was right. Rabia wished that Arthur could change his mind about her.

She rested her hand on Arthur's shoulder and took another swig of rum. "You're a good man Charlie Brown, whatever the rancid hell that means." She looked into his eyes happy to see he looked nervous. She moved closer and parted her lips.

"If I ever die in action, you take my body and you stuff the cold bitch with every lit bomb you can get your hands on and you toss me at the feet of the scumbag's mother who killed me!" she said seriously, and laughed at Arthur's shock.

Arthur nodded in terrified silence, and they split a can of SPAM before succumbing to the warm embrace of sleep.

CHAPTER SEVEN

With morning came nature's imperative, and when on a diet of mostly canned meats it is an imperative that must be taken care of immediately. Arthur and Rabia walked out from the back of the van shortly after waking up, too pre-occupied to take heed of the dust that had buried it.

After a light breakfast of instant mashed potatoes (with a large colored pill and whiskey for Rabia), they set out to manage the damage.

The storm had left nothing behind, but only because it had ground everything into nothing. The dust plains were as barren as they had been the day before. A subtle but familiar green sunrise kissed the dead horizon. Arthur thought it was as beautiful as it was somber and terribly morose.

Arthur wasn't sure what to do with his new found trust for Rabia. This was the first morning he had actually seen her without her hat or sunglasses, and though her afro had been squished by her hat, she looked pretty. More so because she radiated a confidence Arthur was envious of and severely lacked. She half smiled at him, then stuffed a cigarette in her mouth and uttered a string of curses that would make even satan blush and made Arthur queasy. Arthur was *really* not sure of what to do with his new found like or trust.

He had no doubt that Rabia could do her job, and she had already proven to be an asset in their quest to administer a census. But her mood swung to anger quickly, and her appetite for chemicals was hand to mouth. Arthur wasn't sure if he had seen her sober yet. But the most important question had yet to be answered, and it was one that had to be before he could commit to a friendship: would she let him do his job?

Rabia regarded Arthur dully, and stretched her sore muscles. "If we start digging soon, we might be able to get this vicious whale out of the dust before half of the day is gone," she said, dragging two shovels out of the van. She handed one to Arthur then pointed at the van's top. "Once the dust is off, we dig there and get behind it. Getting it upright with just the two of us will be harder than tipping it."

"Do you think we can do it?" Arthur asked.

"If we don't, we have a little under a week's food before we have to play a game of Russian Roulette where the winner eats the loser. After that, pray for the quick death of a raider." Rabia struck ground with her shovel.

Their digging was slower than yesterday, having felt the full burden of it in their tired flesh, but they dug.

The sun hung like a molten disc above the sand-covered plains. Despite the raging ball of fusion that was once worshiped as a god tearing through endless space to reach the earth, it was a cool day. A slight breeze kicked up specks that might once have been the bones of humanity, and tiny whirl-winds danced on the surface of an area that was once preg-nant with plenty.

They dug.

Their shadows shrank, and the former god above them followed its clockwork path forward. So much dogma had been written about man's gods in such a vast amount of time. But in the end man robbed his gods of their final purpose: to end man. And man did it with the same burning fury that fueled their first god, the sun. Maybe the old ways were best, for at least there was without doubt that the sun has no idea of man's plight. It would continue on with or without them.

Still, they dug.

Their shadows started to grow once more. Their first chore done, Rabia jacked the van from its side as far up as it would go, then tied two cords of rope around it. Both man and woman pulled on this cord, laboring to get it back on its tires. When it was finally upright, Rabia patted Arthur on the back, and they collected their gear. Rabia gassed up the van from their supplies, which Arthur made a note of. Soon they would both be inside the van, sipping on precious water and chasing the sun in its constant journey west.

Though the air was heavy with the bodacious madness of Rock 'n' Roll, Rabia kept it at a lower volume, inviting conversation if Arthur felt the need for it. Neither had the strength to talk, but found that sharing silence was no longer awkward. It was, in fact, companionable.

The appetite for socialization was not filled for some time. Rabia drove the lumbering van with the intensity of a banshee. The dust plains eventually gave way to cold scraggly rocks and barren dead trees that splintered upward, now tombstones to their former glory. The van moved up towards a mountain and they climbed in elevation. Light chatter swelled into conversation as the sun slowly dipped into the horizon.

"What exactly is the plan for when we find a poor bastard out here?" Rabia asked.

"You don't know?" Arthur replied, more in annoyance than surprise.

"Forgive me if I have been too busy digging like a lunatic

to do my homework, G-Man. My job is to protect you. I bring you back alive and I don't have to worry about sleeping outside the bunker and wondering where my next meal will come from. What exactly is *your* job?"

Arthur clicked the head of his pen. The mission and its futility weighed on his mind. So far they had survived the cruelties of nature. Man's cruelties were always worse. He repeated the comforting pleasure in his mind, *Only the best,* and honestly tried at that moment to believe that they would make it home.

He licked his dry lips and in no confidence said: "We are going to seek out people, and find out where they live and under what circumstances. The moment we see somebody we are to ask if they have an income and how many people they live with. This will help us ascertain which tax bracket they belong in for collection and auditing purposes."

Rabia put out her cigarette and, because of the dimming light, removed her sunglasses. She looked at Arthur briefly before regarding the road and asked: "What if we don't find anyone?"

"In that case," Arthur replied, "we search until we are halfway through our supplies and then return home".

A mischievous grin crept onto Rabia's face.

"So, let's say we decide to camp out here," she said. "Like the good patriots we are, we decide to take advantage of one of the United Waste's many great national parks." At this she waved a hand towards the corpses of trees and earth that surrounded them. "After a short vacation we return empty handed. No one would be any the wiser."

"Not an option," Arthur said in disdainful impatience. "It is our civic duty and our *job*—"

"Yes, yes," Rabia cut him off. "Dammit, well I tried, you OCD maniac. But finding people means finding trouble. It was a dog eats dog world out there before the dogs had to contend with us eating them." She lit another cigarette.

"This should be easier than an audit," Arthur said, more to assure himself. "The Deputy Commissioner of Operations said himself that we shouldn't expect more than a handful of people."

They were reaching the zenith of the mountain, and stars had begun to shine through the sky once dominated by the sun's hateful glare. Rabia slowed down for the first time in hours. She regarded Arthur with a glance. "Yeah, well, we will have to go looking for that handful tomorrow. It's getting dark. We should get this whale off the road and out of sight, find a comfortable place to sleep."

She turned the van into a small clearing. Arthur made no objection. He was tired from the day's labor and was happy to be able to stretch his legs and eat before having a well-earned sleep.

The moon, man's other old god, had replaced the sun and taken its turn to reign the sky. The earth that imprisoned it in a gravitational tether finally as barren, almost as dead. The moon's soft glow lit up the clearing, which helped Arthur and Rabia navigate their new campsite. Arthur relished being able to walk, his legs now flowing with newly circulated blood. They came to a large horseshoe of boulders. This had the benefit of keeping them out of sight from the road, but it obscured their view of the land. Before Arthur could regard these boulders, Rabia was already climbing the top of one to scan the horizon. It was hard for Arthur not to admire her under the soft glow of the moon.

In a moment, Rabia had climbed to the top of a boulder, hands on her hips in triumph. But then, rather suddenly, her hips stiffened and her arms dropped to her sides. "Holy soul ripping terror," she uttered, and then with a demented urgency, she yelled for Arthur. "Get your paper-filing ass up here, G-Man! NOW!"

Arthur was nowhere as skilled at climbing as Rabia, but with a few fumbles and awkward footing he was able to get up the old rock and sit down next to her.

It didn't take long for him to see it.

Out in the distance, miles from the bottom of the other side of the mountain, were lights.

Not just a few, but a couple dozen. They were far off glimmers in a gulf of darkness, but they were there.

Arthur's heart sank faster than a U-boat being spotted by a destroyer.

"Does this look like a handful of people to you?" Rabia said harshly. "My God, man! That is a village, maybe even a city of people down there."

Arthur's gut reaction was to squeal in terror as he was faced with the same fate that killed his father. He was looking down into a valley that would bring only doom for him and his new Enforcer. But they had to go down there. It was their job, their duty. It was what Henry S. Boyd expected of him.

"That is going to be a lot more paperwork than I had hoped." Arthur said, morosely. Rabia mimed choking him with great intensity, but as the realization of what was before them hit her, she crossed her arms and Arthur let out an extensive sigh.

"This might be a good thing," Arthur said, trying it aloud to see if he believed it. "If there are that many of them in a stationary settlement like that, then they are probably organized. If they are organized, they might be more amicable to our survey taking."

"There is nothing good about them being organized. If they are organized, then they are organized to defend, and nothing is more threatening to a stationary people like outsiders," Rabia said, calmly. "You still hellbent on doing this?" she asked.

"The taxes from a settlement that large are too big to ignore," Arthur replied. "The Revised National Emergency Operations Guide has standards that can forgive their back taxes, but once the IRS is made aware of them they are subject to current taxes."

"Were you beaten with an abacus as a child?! LOOK AT THAT MONSTER! Those people will eat us alive, and that is not hyperbole! This is not a fucking clerical error to fix, this is life and death!"

"I know," said Arthur, terror gripping his heart.

Rabia jumped down from the boulder. The moment her feet made landfall she walked to the van and downed a hefty amount of Wild Turkey. Arthur followed, but, afraid of the height, he worked his way down slowly. Once he was on the ground, Rabia stopped pulling from the bottle, and looked at Arthur with somber eyes.

"I know that there is no stopping you," she said. "And I can't just go back without you. It would look suspicious and, despite your best efforts, you have grown on me." She said this with disdain. Arthur began to smile, but she cut the head off it. "Grown on me like a rash! This is the dumbest god damn thing we could ever die for!" She took another swig and immediately lit a cigarette. "If we go down there for your demented office errand, we go down there under my lead."

Arthur nodded, and a dreadful silence surrounded them. The quiet was interrupted by a sharp succession of pen clicking. Nothing was playing out the way it should. He should be safe in the bunker, running inventory and perfecting spreadsheets. He knew it wasn't fair to blame the Deputy Commissioner; there was no way for him to know there would be an entire civilization to count. Yet... after seeing just how insanely meticulous Henry S. Boyd was, it was hard not to think that he wasn't capable of an oversight, no matter how small.

Rabia regarded Arthur with a kinder gaze, then took a drag off her cigarette. "We drive halfway down this hateful mountain early tomorrow, at four in the morning, slowly and without headlights. We find a good place to hide the van and then we walk there. Any questions?"

"Why are we walking there?" Arthur said, nearly indignant, his muscles sore from two days of digging.

"Because they'll see us driving from miles away, G-Man, we don't exactly want to sneak up on them, but we don't want to loudly announce that we are coming either. Besides our little federal bunker, no one drives except caravans and land pirates, and *one* of those is enough to get a town locked and loaded. Any more questions?"

Arthur shook his head.

"Good. We bring only the bare essentials and we make no mention of transportation. Under no circumstances do you tell them about our van. If they haven't killed us, and against all odds you count those heads without me having to pull the trigger, then we come back."

Arthur listened studiously. "I think we only have enough forms for that settlement, so we can go home after that," he said.

"YOU GOD DAMN BETTER BELIEVE WE GO HOME AFTER THAT!" Rabia screeched. "Mother of a filthy swine! I don't care if you only fill out half of them, we turn our tails and we run crying *home*. Do you understand?!" Arthur smiled, realizing that Rabia's yelling was only theatrics, so long as she didn't have a gun in her hand.

Then she grabbed her shotgun.

"I'm going to check our perimeter. We sleep in the van again tonight. We leave no sign of camp." Rabia said, walking toward the entrance of the horseshoe, paying no mind to Arthur's pen clicking.

Beneath the dread, and behind the deathly nervousness, there was something brewing within Arthur that only another bureaucrat could understand. This was not something that he could admit to Rabia, and in fact it was hard enough to admit to himself. This feeling, this terrible and almost evil feeling he'd had? Giddiness. Giddiness because there were blank forms to be filled out that would set in motion a new tax era for the United Wastes. It was like a burning sensation, one that would only numb once there were names and numbers written down in official black ink.

Druids of old wrote down sigils that would otherwise devour their psyche. The only difference here is that maybe the sigils were useful.

He and Rabia had more in common then he first suspected. It manifested differently, but without a doubt, they were both driven by a madness. And they both craved more of it.

CHAPTER EIGHT

The smell of morning dew had mixed with ash, because 'wet dust' was simply not horrifying enough for the United Wastes. Light had started to peek over the mountain, and rays shone through dead branches. The dead woods were like a series of skeleton hands, each reaching out to a sky as barren as they.

Once, the sounds of birds were reassuring. Once, it was a sign of danger if the birds had gone quiet. Now, the sounds of birds would be foreign, even wrong. Now, it was always quiet because there was always danger.

Reaching the very edge of this macabre forest, Arthur McDowell and Rabia Duke walked without uttering a word. They had left the van behind them hours ago. Smoke had begun to rise from the settlement ahead, some lights still flickering in the sleepy morning. Whoever was out there was likely making breakfast. The thought of a warm meal was at once pleasing, but was something that they could not risk. If they made it out alive, they would have to do so without the settlement knowing which direction they had come from. They both settled on a can of grapefruit.

Rabia led, grumpy from a hangover. It swam in her mind with a mixture of shame and anxiety, but not regret. Her shotgun was not slung over her back, and instead found itself held in her hands. It was used to being held in anger, even fear, but this was a new feeling for it: It was being held in uncertainty. This was not a posture Rabia had often.

Arthur was not far behind her. His black tie was neat, his hair combed. Despite two days of digging, he was still the face of the IRS and was as presentable as the United Wastes had let him be. Every agent of the IRS kept this in mind: they were likely the only federal employees that anyone would meet. They were likely the only federal employees left. They were not just representing the IRS; they were representing the United States government. No matter how the denizens of the wastes felt about being taxed, Arthur worked for them. He was, at the end of the day, a civil servant. Today he would meet any unknown terror with a smile, and he would be candid with those who grew up with only a vague under-standing of what government looked like. It was his job to.

After clearing the forest, Rabia looked back at Arthur and tossed him a canteen. "Let's take a water break and watch them for a moment," she said. "Our caravan always waited to go into a town until after the smoke settled. We wait 'till they are done eating, they'll probably be in a better mood, and less likely to want to eat us." She sat down on a stump. Arthur walked toward her and thought about sitting on the stump's other edge, but opted to stand instead.

"You remind me of my ex, Melody," Rabia said after watching Arthur's indecisiveness. "She was about as anxious to be near me as you are."

Arthur gave a lighthearted chuckle. "Even your ex-girl-friend was anxious around you?" he smiled.

"Girlfriend? Christ no. Ex sex-slave," Rabia corrected. Arthur looked back in mild terror. "I picked her up at a small slavers' camp, traded an automatic rifle for her."

Arthur responded with silence.

"She left me amicably. Freedom will do that . . . What about you G-Man? You got someone at home?"

Stalling, Arthur drank some water. When this didn't suffice to lengthen his stall, he handed the canteen back to Rabia and waited for her to finish drinking as if it prevented her from hearing him. He could not tell if she was just merely curious, or actually interested. It occurred to him that maybe he was interested in her, and that was surprising to him.

"Office fraternization is frowned upon," Arthur replied, finally, absentmindedly clicking the top of his pen.

"Bummer," Rabia said with a half smile. She turned her gaze towards their destination and frowned sharply at it. "Don't go dying on me today, G-Man, I like working with you. You're polite, and fucking nobody is polite in this world."

Arthur did not know how to reciprocate, so instead he hesitantly patted her back and said nothing.

After a minute's rest, they were both back on their feet, and the distance closed.

As the sun moved higher into the blue sky, the dew began to evaporate, leaving no more moisture anywhere, save the canteens in their gear. The smoke that raged upwards in the village had stopped. There was nothing in the air but dryness. Rocks crunched under their feet, and when Arthur could not bear to look at their destination, he stared down at the ground. It offered him no hope.

They were close enough now to see the giant wall surrounding the settlement. It was a mixture of sheet metal, and cut trees from the forest, circling the perimeter of the area from end to end. There was an entrance wide enough for a four-lane road, which Arthur and Rabia aimed toward. Save for the occasional shattered looking roof from an old suburban building, there was nothing to see at their level.

It was impossible to see beyond the wall. What it protected, or hid, was anyone's guess.

Despite its unnerving mystery, the wall was a comfort to them. Rabia saw a town that wanted to be protected; walls kept people out, and at the very least that meant that they were not raiders. To Arthur, the wall was exciting, because it meant at least one person in the settlement was employed as a carpenter. His finger itched to write down an official, and normal sounding, position of employment on form D-61.

Neither said a word while they walked, Arthur out of fear of being heard, and Rabia presumably because of a pounding headache from her hangover.

The settlement grew in size as they drew closer. They were now far away enough to see two men, possibly guards, at the entrance. It was a certainty that those men saw them as well. This was it. An Auditor, conscripted into a Census Administrator, and a surly, never-sober Enforcer had come to their first people in the unknown region to which they were assigned. *Only the best* Arthur repeated in his head, and then *Godspeed.*

The men did not look mean; they looked psychotic. The detached look of cruelty crept from the eyes of one, while the cold stare of poor intelligence leapt out of the other. Both of these eyes would be better housed in lizards.

The clothing that wasn't scavenged was instead made from sheet metal and bleached human bones. They looked like they were wearing the feverish carapaces of beetles made from junk. The one with the cruel eyes clutched a rifle covered in duct tape at the grip, almost phallic-like; over his shoulder, the other carried a cricket bat with nails beaten into it. These two looked like the spirit of the post-nuclear apocalypse personified. If man was twisted before the war, it was a twistedness with a polished veneer that was foreign to these two. Violence was self-expression now, and these two? These two were artists.

"She's mine!" the one with the bat said, staring lustfully at Rabia. "I like 'em like I like my water, black and screaming."

Rabia stared stoically, her sunglasses hiding a gaze more terrifying than either of these men were capable of.

The man with the rifle nudged the other.

"Oi! Remember what the Colonel said, 'be nice to customers'. Ya can have her if they don' buy anything," the one with the rifle said, then looked up at Rabia. "You are gonna buy something, right pretty miss?" His mouth widened not unlike a smile, revealing rotten and missing teeth. The few that were still there had been filed to fangs.

One misstep here meant death. This was a bridge made out of thin china set across a poisonous ravine. This situation called for precision, wit, and a little bit of luck.

So instead Arthur administered the census.

"Yes! Hello! I am an agent of the IRS," Arthur said, "I am here for a quick census."

There was a quick look of recognition from the man with the rifle. The man with the cricket bat looked on with an almost violent stupidity.

"Whaz that mean?" the man with the bat said.

"A census probably hasn't been done in this area in a generation, so no reason to be embarrassed if you have not heard about one," Arthur said to two men who were not embarrassed. "The IRS is simply counting the populace for tax purposes, I am here to help you fine men fill out a questionnaire about your living conditions."

Arthur's nervousness was gone. Rabia looked on, surprised to see a wave of confidence wash over him. It was a suicidal confidence, but one she admired nonetheless. He was in his element.

The guarded posture of the men had eased. The one with the bat lowered his weapon. "You want to ask us questions?" he said in a childlike tone.

"Yes that's right, just a number of questions for the IRS database. We can start now if you would like?"

Before the man with the bat could answer, a third man, shirtless and covered in poorly drawn tattoos of snakes walked by behind the gate. The man with the rifle called out to him. "Oi! We got 'nother one of them sense-ass guys, see what the Colonel wants!" The man in the snake tattoos, which looked more like garden hoses with eyes, looked back and nodded, then disappeared back behind the gate. Rabia shifted her weight.

She could see better into the settlement now, but much was still obscured. She removed a flask from her back pocket and took a swig, then offered it to the guards as a peace offering. The more casual the guards became the better. The man with the rifle snatched it greedily and drank voraciously, then passed it to the other. They continued to look at Rabia, their gaze lingering on her naked legs with half open mouths, but the alcohol had simmered the intensity. No one here was friends yet, but this was miles better than where they were only a minute ago.

Arthur pulled out his clipboard and, with an official click of his pen, looked at the man with the bat. "Let me get your last name first and your first next with your middle initial last," he said. This was met with silent bewilderment.

"Huh?"

"Ah, what ah, what is your name?"

"Dumb Dick Rick," the man with the bat responded, with a wink at Rabia. She would shoot his dick first if this went down. *Oh yes,* she thought, *you'll get circumcised with gunpowder you dumb Nazi fuck.* She smiled at him with cruel anticipation.

Arthur filled out the form *Rick, Dumb D.* and was about to move on to the next question when two men carrying a large cage passed by the gate.

Smiling at the men, Rabia placed her hand on Arthur's shoulder. "Allow me a private moment with my colleague. Feel free to finish that whiskey," She gently turned Arthur around. "*Get the fuck over here,*" she whispered.

She led him a hundred paces along the side of the wall, then stopped and looked at him with fear. "As your Enforcer, I advise that we *get the fuck out of Dodge*. These men are slavers. We won't die here, Arthur, we will be caught and sold here. That is a future of brutal rape for both of us." She cocked her red shotgun. "We walk along this wall to the corner until we're out of their sight and then take a different route to the van."

Arthur knew she was right. Slavers were worse than raiders, and even land pirates. Raiders would kill you, not always quickly but your pain would end. Slavers bought and sold people as workers, sex objects, and sometimes as food, but your life would go on without freedom and with a lot of agony. It was a future of the worst kind. This was *absolutely* the worse case scenario for their journey, if they went any further it would end here, and a life of random cruelty would be the only forecast ahead of them.

But Arthur's form was not completely filled.

"No," Arthur said. "I am a civil servant and I have a duty—"

"You OCD bastard! Those men were staring at you just as lustfully as they were at me, Pretty-lips! We go, now!"

"I thought you were a professional," Arthur accused with his arms crossed.

"I *am* a professional, a freelance professional, and I intend to stay free."

"The Revised National Emergency Operations guide stipu—"

"To hell with your guide, man!"

"I have to do my job," Arthur finished. Rabia saw a commitment in his eyes; it was the same look she had seen in a wrist cutter a few years ago. Arthur moved past her, clipboard in hand. There was no arguing with a bureaucrat. She followed behind slowly, keeping a substantial distance. Her naked legs, a necessity for the outdoors suddenly made her feel vulnerable. She had grown up with a healthy fear of men and had learned to fight better than any, but when outnumbered by an entire town, well, then vulnerable is exactly as she should feel.

The two guards had multiplied to six.

Arthur's hand began to tremble. Rabia's breath was shallow.

"Sorry for the delay Mr. Rick, my partner and I were discussing how best to proceed to make sure that your experience of the census is a positive one," Arthur said. The four new men looked no less savage. If they were a band, they would be the kind that threw cats at brick walls and insisted it was music.

The man with the snake tattoos was among them.

They spread out slowly, creating a u-shape around Arthur.

There was no time to turn back now. Arthur was at their mercy, and mercy was a strange word never uttered on their tongues.

The confidence that was once at Arthur's command had peed itself.

Arthur clicked his pen and winced at the sound. The men looked hungry, with lust, for violence, and to fill every haunting desire of their id.

"D-Do you all live together? If you all have lived in the same place since before April—"Arthur stammered, his voice now bordering on a squeal.

The man with the snake tattoos cleared his throat, silencing Arthur's ramblings. He slowly pulled a machete from his back and smiled. "Thas 'nuff of your questions. The Colonel wants a private consultation with ya," he said.

The man with the rifle pointed its muzzle at Rabia. "Alone," he added.

Arthur's pen clicked at a rapid-fire rate.

"We are a partnership," Rabia said, shotgun raised. "If he goes, I go."

"Nothin' doin', pretty miss," said the man with the rifle. "The Colonel gets what he wants 'round here in Slaver City, so put down your gun all nice like. The Colonel just wants to talk about your sense-ass."

Rabia expected Arthur to turn around, but instead, pen and clipboard at the ready, he said "The Colonel, he's your head of household, yes?"

Goodbye, you kind, polite, batshit insane bastard, Rabia thought helplessly as she lowered her weapon.

Dumb Dick Rick had a look of brutal confusion. "The Colonel is the colonel of Slaver City!" he barked.

Under NAME Arthur wrote: *Colonel,* under occupation he wrote: *Colonel.* Four of the six men had closed the u-shape, now surrounding him completely and cutting him off from Rabia. The other two stood in front of Rabia. The men behind Arthur pushed him forward ushering him away. He obliged without contest. Looking over his shoulder, Arthur could only see Rabia's hat, the word 'Professional' written across it, through the wall of men behind him. *She let me do my job,* he thought. The phrase *Guns go up? Don't frown! Fall down!*

ran through his head like an endless scrolling marquee, advice that was totally useless now.

The four men pushed Arthur into the city, leaving the remaining two with Rabia. With his view no longer obscured by the walls, Arthur saw a large wooden pole, probably once used to hold up a school crossing sign, but which now had a new purpose. The top of it was sharpened into a spike, and it no longer carried the municipal safety sign it once bore, instead carried a new sign.

Punctured by the spike was the head of a red-haired man, his face frozen in a permanent scream.

It was the head of the agent who had delivered Henry S. Boyd's coffee late.

CHAPTER NINE

It was a grim throne for an even grimmer king.

This was the sort of thing that CEOs before The War could only dream about making for a symbol of power. It was far more effective than a red muscle car and far more perverse than filling that car up with girls barely turned women. It was not something that anyone alive then with power had dared to make because it was simply too honest and overt in its symbolism. These men of power from old would have immediately been ousted as the psychopaths that they were had they sat atop this monster. They did not dare then.

Now? Now was an age where team building exercises meant killing wild dogs with scavenged junk. Now was an age where men literally chained young girls to the hoods of their 'death-mobiles'. Now was an age where power play was simply a pull of the trigger. It was a renaissance for psychopaths, and this throne? Well, this throne was the motherfucking Mona Lisa.

An equal amount of human teeth and spent bullet casings

spiraled up a concrete base. So tightly packed were these teeth and shells that one would assume that there was no concrete behind them holding it together. They would be wrong in this assumption, but only because the smallest amount of concrete that could have possibly shone through had. This base formed into a chariot, with the large molars of men and women and the shells of high caliber bullets at the bottom petering up to the baby teeth of children and smaller casings at the top. Two long and thick chains lay limp at the side, and monster truck wheels that the base of the throne sat on were held in place by cinderblocks. The base was three feet high, and although teeth were easy to find in any of the many cities now turned into a radioactive crater, one got the very distinct feeling that the artist behind this beast had used only the freshest of ingredients.

The cherry on top was not the seat, no, because the artist designed it as a two-piece sculpture, one that could be separated, but needs both halves to bring it all together. The seat was an old leather Cadillac driver's seat, the piece that completed the throne was the man who sat on it: The Colonel.

Overweight, this slug of a man sat on his throne with the bored listlessness reserved for only the most slothful. The lower jaws of men protruded out of the toes of his black boots. Whatever material his pants were, they had tattered to a web-like structure over the metal casings he wore on his hips, culminating into a foul looking codpiece. A white suit jacket, although torn and fringed at the elbows, was actually bleached and sat on top of an equally white vest and collared shirt. A long flab of skin, riddled with tumors fell from his chin, creating a wattle that a chicken would cringe at. It should have obscured the confederate flag bolo tie underneath it, but being the unsightly thing that it was, it was hard not to notice every detail in and around it.

This was The Colonel, a man so cruel that the slavers around him declared him king, without question. His brutal throne and his decaying body on top of the ruble of an old fast food restaurant. He sat there like a plucked and mutilated rooster observing from a roost of madness.

Arthur wanted to ask him about his deductibles. Old habits.

Arthur was pushed toward The Colonel, albeit still around 20 feet away. The men who had 'escorted' him there turned away, either out of fear or disgust. Or both.

A voice like buttered grease boomed from the Colonel "You been asking questions you shoulda been asking me, boy!"

"Definitely, sir. We can start with you and then move on to the others!" Arthur bellowed back.

"What?" The Colonel said.

"Should I come closer?!"

"Yeah, that'd be nice!"

Arthur obliged. The four men who brought him there stayed behind, still avoiding the gaze of the cruel rooster. Once he was within five feet, a terribly close proximity for a smell that was as equally horrid as the throne, Arthur pulled up his clipboard. "You wanted to see me, sir?" Arthur said.

"Yeah, I heard you were goin' 'round taking a sense-ass in my little neighborhood," said The Colonel. "The last two guys, see, one was too quiet, didin' say much I wanted to hear, and the other? Well, he talked right too much for my likin'. One of dem has their head on a pike now, can you guess which one?"

Arthur, confined to his fate, was less scared than he should have been. "Was it the talkative one?" he said with genuine curiosity.

The Colonel laughed at this, a sound that had more wheezing than mirth. "You know, I don't remember! It was only a couple of days ago, and this 'ol head of mine, well it might as well have been a hundred years!" Arthur expected him to stroke his wattle like it was a long beard. "How you like my shoes, boy?" The Colonel continued. "Made 'em out of the hired guns they brought."

Arthur's heart collapsed into his bowels. The thought of Rabia meeting the same fate threatened tears. He fought them away, trying his best to act professionally.

"I think they are pretty trendy for a man of power in the United Wastes," Arthur said with hollow commitment.

"You think so?" The Colonel sounded surprised. "No one 'round here 'preciates all my efforts." he said, his hand creeping up to his chin.

He's gonna do it, Arthur thought with a dreadfully pleasant expectation.

"I know why you are here, boy, so lemme tell you what..." The Colonel said, now stroking his wattle. *I KNEW IT* Arthur's mind howled in a mix of victory and gross despair. "...For every question you ask me on that there sense-ass, I git to ask you one myself. Does that sound fair to you, boy?" Arthur tried not to gag as The Colonel ran his fingers over a particularly large tumor.

Having conceded he would not be alive to administer the census, Arthur agreed to this proposition enthusiastically. He nodded his head vehemently and clicked his pen. The tables *name* and *occupation* were preemptively filled out, so Arthur moved on to the next question, crossing out *apartment, house,* and *mobile home* and updating with what he felt was appropriate.

"Mr. The Colonel, sir, is this 'Terror Throne' A: Owned by you or someone in your Thronehold with a mortgage or loan? B: Owned by you or someone in this Thronehold free and clear? C: Rented, or D: Occupied without payment or rent?" Arthur asked, reading off of his modified form D-61.

The Colonel stroked his flab contemplatively. "You know, before now I jus' called it my sittin' chair, but I reckon I like Terror Throne much better. Good on you, boy! But I own this throne wholesale."

Arthur put a checkmark on B.

"My turn," The Colonel said. "How many of y'all's scouts are there in my neck of the woods?"

Arthur looked up from his clipboard, concerned. "I don't know, but I honestly didn't think two others would make it out here, so at least 3?"

It was hard to tell if this pleased The Colonel.

"Mr. The Colonel," Arthur said, continuing with the task in hand, "were there any additional people staying at your Terror Throne on or before April 1st?" This seemed like an unlikely scenario, and even he would be the first to admit that. It was hard to imagine anyone sitting on top of the throne with The Colonel, but it was also hard for Arthur to imagine that he would be talking to a man with a mutated wattle, so...perspective?

The Colonel's eyes indicated boredom. His hand returned to the top of his chin to begin stroking his unsightly flab again. "You know, I don' think anyone here really knows what month it is. We sold off a woman named April not too long ago, but no, son, I'm the only bastard that sits here."

"No...additional...people..." Arthur read aloud as he marked a check on the form.

"My turn," the Colonel said. "When does your gang of raiders plan on getting at us?"

The question surprised Arthur. He shifted his weight awkwardly, his throat parched more than ever. "Sorry?" was all that he could manage.

Rage filled The Colonel's eyes, a molten hot stare that threatened to lay waste on everything it met, yet the rest of his body remained slothful and relaxed. When he spoke,

Arthur was surprised to find the hideous man's voice steady and calm, which only served to make him all the more terrifying.

"Let's be honest with each other, boy, this here 'sense-ass' is intelligence gatherin', it's a poor attempt, but we all know what the IRS does, they are the Iron Raider's Society, the meanest and largest gang east of here. You're here to count up my men to see how many troops I got. Now, when does your king plan on doing the raidin'?"

"I-I can see why you are confused Mr. The Colonel, sir, but the IRS stands for—"

"I DON'T GIVE A RAT'S ASS WHAT IT STANDS FOR!" he bellowed, his voice borrowing some of the rage from his eyes. Arthur winced. "We know what you do. You steal from job creators, job creators like me. Not enough to ruin me, no, you're smart 'bout that. You know that if I thrive and make calories as a business owner, that you can come back for more! Your army is gonna come to my front door at some point! WHEN?!"

"I-I don't know," Arthur said. Some of the rage subsided in The Colonel's eyes. Arthur wondered if he stored his anger in his wattle.

"I believe you," The Colonel said, "grunt like you shouldn't know anyways. This'll go much quicker if we don't bullshit, son. Now, I think it's your turn for a question."

Arthur looked at his clipboard. The next question said *Is Person 1 of Hispanic, Latino, or Spanish origin?* but Arthur wasn't sure if he dared to ask that question to a warlord sporting a hate symbol on his bolo tie. Suddenly, and for the first time in Arthur's bureaucratic career, the questionnaire did not seem to matter. Did everyone in the United Wastes feel this way about the IRS? He had heard Rabia say much of the same things (except she wasn't a monster who sold people and claimed to be a "job creator"). Arthur was merely doing his job, but just how different *was* he to a raider? Also: weren't there more important questions to ask?

"What will happen to my Enforcer?" Arthur asked, his frightened emotions not hidden.

"Lookie here!" The Colonel said, shifting his weight in his morbid throne for the first time. "Now *there's* a question worth askin'! If what my boys are sayin' 'bout her is right, why, I reckon that pretty black thing will sell off right quick!" The Colonel licked his lips. "If she don't fight back, that is."

He had his chance. She had practically begged Arthur to turn around, and begging was something he figured she did not do often. Wouldn't it have been nice to just camp out with a brutal, foul-mouthed, intelligent and beautiful woman? Hell, she had somehow tolerated, and even liked Arthur which was rare. Instead, he had gotten them captured. He had ensured that his new friend's greatest fears would be played out every day. And for what?

A census.

"My turn," The Colonel said, folding his meaty hands over his metal codpiece. "How many of y'all are there? And don't bullshit me."

Arthur could lie, but it occurred to him that he was now the third IRS agent to be interrogated, so his numbers should really match the others. But more importantly, the public did have a right to the number of people the IRS employed, being a federal institution.

"Hundreds," Arthur said, looking down at his feet.

Does person 1 sometimes live or stay somewhere else? His form prompted next. Instead, Arthur asked: "What...what will you do with me?"

"Lookit that!" The Colonel said, slapping his knees. "Now I git to be the one who says I don't know!" Laughter crept out of his mouth, his wattle jiggling. "You been real nice, boy, I'll give you that. I don't think I'm gonna kill you. I reckon I'll do with you what I did with the old man, it's not often that free inventory walks in here!"

The Colonel stuck two sausage-like fingers in his mouth and whistled shrill and fierce. Arthur was suddenly aware of how much space was around him that he could probably run and not get caught, but could he run and not get shot? And was that better than getting caught?

A man wearing nothing but a loincloth and biker's helmet crawled through one of the fast-food restaurant's windows from a side that had not collapsed. He was emaciated-looking and, like The Colonel, he was also riddled with tumors. A large book was tied to his back with belts. He looked like some sort of mutant turtle.

He climbed up to The Colonel and got down on all fours before him, facing away. It was like the book was a table top and he was the legs. The Colonel rose, with less effort than Arthur would have guessed, opened the book, and removed a pen from his codpiece. "Looks like I git to write something down too!" he said, clicking his pen. He licked a sausage finger on his other hand and rapidly flicked through the pages.

The title of the book read "Inventory and Sales".

Despite the heavy portents of doom weighing down on him, Arthur could not but help feel a little excited to see this book. An insane urge to audit the book itched inside of the lining of his skull. Old habits.

The Colonel found the page that he was looking for. "Day two hundred, admit one slave, free inventory," He said, looking down at Arthur with a cruel smile.

The guards behind him started making their way closer, surrounding him like they had done before.

The man with the rifle was only about five feet away now. Arthur's mind volunteered *Guns go up? Don't frown! Fall down!* But that only worked if there was an Enforcer.

His indecisiveness destroyed what little hope he had in running, in dying quickly. He was now completely surrounded.

The Colonel raised his hand and the guards stopped. With dark mirth, The Colonel looked at Arthur. "I git one more question!" he said, kicking away the emaciated table, the jaw of a dead Enforcer flying off his boot from the force of the kick. "Why do you do what you do, boy?" he asked.

There were a million answers that, just a day ago, Arthur felt passionate about. It was his civic duty, his job; it was something he liked doing; he was born into it; somebody needed to collect taxes. He had done his job without question. He had done everything he was supposed to do and instead of being rewarded with the promotion of safety that was owed to him he was standing at the foot of a psychopath in charge of monsters. He had spent his life counting numbers, and now he would be sold off, and *he would be counted*.

"I don't know," Arthur said.

The Colonel laughed.

"That's what I thought, boy, that's what I thought." The Colonel looked down at his guards. "Take him to the south fields and put him in a cage next to the old one we caught yesterday. You two catch that hired gun of his and bring her to me first." There was lust in his eyes.

The men obliged. Of the four guards that had escorted Arthur earlier, only the man with the poorly drawn tattoos and Dumb Dick Rick remained. Dumb Dick Rick shoved Arthur forward.

He did not fight it. The two men did not have to force Arthur along. Arthur was despondent now that he had a new career of slavery ahead of him, and thought bitterly that he had been one his entire life.

The fast food restaurant behind him grew smaller but the bloated rooster's gaze could still be felt.

At least my father had the sense to die in this world, Arthur thought, soberly. He hugged his clipboard to his chest in despair. Then they took it away from him.

CHAPTER TEN

The setting sun offered great relief to the field of cages. The rage it had been beating into the hot earth was finally subsiding and the blood orange smear across the dead horizon radiated a sense of peace to the slaves. It was the only beautiful thing most of them had seen in months.

The rows of cages were uniform following a strict grid, yet the cages themselves were anything but. Some were the kind of cage one would expect to find holding an animal; professionally built, made of steel bars and definitely from before The War. Some were built from scrap, a mixture of chain link fence welded around rusty car frames. Some were just boxes of sheet metal with penny-sized air holes drilled into them. No matter their shape, they all held living and breathing people, their numbers in the high dozens.

Arthur had been put to work to "earn his keep" before finding himself in the remnants of a van turned cage. He was marched from one side of Slaver City where the slavers' well had been dug, and forced to carry two five gallon buckets of water across to the cage fields, a good mile away, and dump them into a large trough. He did this over and over as the sun hammered the earth with cosmic rays. He wasn't allowed a single drop for himself.

The trough of water stood dead center between the rows of cages, and to Arthur's great dismay was not for the slaves. It was for the guards; a place where they could openly drink to diminish the hopes of the men and women they held captive. A slave was only allowed water after they "earned their keep" and when customers arrived.

Arthur sat down in his cage as soon as he was thrown into it. The van that the cage was built out of was cut in half with the back portion stripped of all seats, doors and windows, and then wrapped with a thick chain link. It was directly opposite the front half, made in the same fashion. Despite the setting sun, the cage's metal floor was still hot, but Arthur's tired and aching muscles had voted that the discomfort was worth it to endure.

This was all his fault.

Sure, he was just doing what he was told to do, but at the end of the day, he still chose to do it.

This was going to be his life until he was sold. The frightening part? This was better than being sold. He had already heard rumors from the guards who marched him up and down Slaver City that many buyers bought slaves to dig for food. There was a sort of mad gold rush fever for canned goods that had been buried by the radioactive blasts of fusion bombs. It seemed unlikely to Arthur that anyone would find anything near the craters, and if they did it was probably awash with radioactivity. This did not matter. If the slave found nothing, the hole was usually too deep to get out of, and they would become bait for something else looking for food. If nothing came? If nothing took to the bait, and their masters had nothing to collect from their efforts, well they could always just eat the slave.

A guard came to the trough. He was covered head to toe

in sheet metal armor and was shorter than Arthur. He turned his back, stood at the trough for a stunted moment and then left. Arthur's parched throat made his tongue feel like sandpaper. He turned away from the torturous trough, and that was when he saw him...

Across from him, in the other half of the van, where a steering wheel should be, was an old man. An impossibly old man. He wore a collard white shirt, a black tie, and his badge read: Commissioner for Operations, Jack Dewitt.

Blood flushed to his slugged muscles, adrenaline poured through his heart, and Arthur shot to the edge of his cage closest to the old man. This was his boss; this was Henry Boyd's boss! The highest-ranking IRS official Arthur had ever laid eyes on, now stuck in a cage, like him.

"Sir?" Arthur said. "Commissioner Dewitt!" he yelled, not caring if the guards had heard him.

The commissioner turned his ancient head and met Arthur's eyes with his own tired grey ones. "So," the Commissioner said, "looks like we have another casualty for my trap."

Arthur blinked. Then he blinked again. When he thought of saying something, he elected to blink once more instead. "What?" was the only intelligible thing he could offer.

"What's your name, agent?" Dewitt asked impatiently.

"Arthur McDowell sir, Auditor #A24."

"And now you're a Census Taker I suppose?"

"Yes sir!"

"Me too."

This didn't make sense.

"I've heard of you, seen your file passed around, I'm sorry about that promotion, Mr. McDowell," Dewitt said, moving closer. "We had great hopes for you; it was a shame to see you go off in the first wave. How is it that I have gotten here before you? You left a full 12 hours before me."

"Radioactive sandstorm sir, forced us to dig down and sit

it out for most of the second day," Arthur said. There were a million questions swimming like caffeinated sharks in his head, but the most selfish one came out first: "You knew of my promotion?"

"Of course," Dewitt answered. "I personally thought there was no one better for it. After you were chosen in Boyd's surprise 'lottery' for the conscription, the position still had to be filled. Went to a man by the name of Ralph Siemens. It was very unfortunate." Dewitt clutched at the chain-link fence holding him in. "Not that it matters now."

It did. He understood Dewitt's sentiment; there was no future for them now, but it mattered because it was a promise. It mattered because it was the only shred of hope Arthur had held on to going into this mission. If he got back, he was promoted. Period. But to hear that it was immediately awarded to Ralph, no less than 12 hours later (and given the efficiency of the IRS, likely immediately after) was like grinding salt covered glass into an already festering wound.

The two guards that had brought him here, the man with the poorly drawn snake tattoos, and Dumb Dick Rick, were now at the trough. Each stuck their head in and drank voraciously. When they had had their fill, the man in the tattoos pulled out a knife and started to sharpen it with his belt. They clearly intended to stay for a bit, let the slaves know who was in charge.

Dewitt lowered his voice. "I'm sorry you got caught up in this. Boyd wanted me out of the way, always has. There wasn't anything he was unwilling to do to get my position, but it was mine to have." His tired eyes met Arthur's once more. "The Revised National Emergency Operations Guide clearly states that anyone, no matter their pay grade or position, can be reassigned to carry out essential operations. The Guide also states census taking as 'essential'."

The rest did not need to be said aloud. Henry S. Boyd had initiated this census to get what he wanted and damn the consequences. The man that Arthur had looked up to, his hero, had purposefully sent an unknown amount of men to their deaths so that he could take advantage of a loophole that would allow him to move up in the agency. The bureaucrat in Arthur respected the calculus, but the man in him wept at the coldness.

"The two of us are finished," Dewitt said, then collapsed to a sitting position in despondent misery and physical pain. "Thank you for your service."

"Keep quiet over there! Don't talk durin' our break!" Dumb Dick Rick yelled. But there was no need. The Commissioner had lost interest in Arthur, now confined to his fate. As for Arthur, well, his existential terror was too deep to move him to words.

The last civil place on the planet, well, it just let psychopaths climb the ladder of authority with a cold distance. The system that he grew up in, that he believed in, truly and without compromise - what difference was there between it and the terrible hierarchy here? Both Henry S. Boyd and The Colonel had killed men to get to where they are, but at least The Colonel had the decency to throttle those men with his own sausage-like fingers. Boyd had just filed a form. He lied to Arthur's face. This was supposed to be easy, there was supposed to be no one here, a tribe at most. Instead there was a death trap, and Arthur had stepped into it, willingly!

"Where'd you git those tats?" Dumb Dick Rick asked the other guard, pointing at the striped garden hoses with poorly drawn circles for eyes. "Those snakes are sick."

"Forced a man at gunpoint to do 'em," the tattooed man replied. "Said it'd take him hours, I told him to do them before I was done eating my breakfast!"

"Alpha male," Dumb Dick Rick approved without emotion, fist bumping the other.

"Alpha male for sure," the tattooed man agreed. "Only took 'bout twenty minutes, but I had been done with my can of beans by then, so I blew his fucking head off once he was done. Probably the best work of his life." He looked at his permanent doodles and smiled with admiration.

More men came to the trough, each with a weapon holstered or slung over their shoulder. A couple of them had slabs of cooked, greasy meat in their hands. There were 11 of them total, gathered around the trough as if it were an office water cooler, and each one took a long drink before leaning against it. The group was testosterone mixed with an ignorance that almost had integrity. Arthur looked on. These men were proud, brutal, stupid and arrogant. Was this what man had reverted to as a result of society collapsing, or had he always been this way, only now he no longer had to hide it?

Dewitt gave Arthur a sidelong look, still sitting in defeat. He recognized the look of disapproval in Arthur's face. "You weren't alive before the bombs fell," Dewitt said in a hushed tone. "We were always like that, only interested in covering our own insecurities with a false sense of superiority. If someone thought you were weak, then you picked on or blamed someone that was different than you: women, different races, different sexualities, hell, anyone and everyone that wasn't close to you. The only difference between them now and then is that then we didn't have an excuse for it, but we did it anyways."

Dewitt raised a hand over his shoulder and clutched the fence. "I saw that in Boyd. The only thing that gives that man pleasure is being above someone else. I kept my position for as long as I did so he wouldn't get that satisfaction."

A few of the guards had spread from the trough, but not far from it. A few of them leaned against the cages, knowing that the slave within would not dare to grab them. It was like dogs pissing to mark their territory, and now that Arthur thought about it, it wasn't a stretch to see one of them do exactly that. The guard that was head to toe in sheet metal had returned. He leaned casually on Arthur's cage. Dewitt stopped speaking at once, not wanting to push his luck.

Arthur wanted his promotion because it meant safety, and in all honesty he would have been happy to stay there. Or so he thought. He had never been in charge of someone else. Would that power have gone to his head? If he somehow did get home and got the promotion that he deserved, how long would it take before power had poisoned his soul? He had always run fantasies in his mind's eye of sending Ralph's smug face off to his death. Wasn't this what Boyd had done to Dewitt?

Was civility a luxury to mask the rancid monkeys that they truly were?

The sun had almost completely set and a cool breeze washed over the caged people. It was the closest thing they would get to refreshment.

"Anyone else hot?" Dumb Dick Rick boomed at no one in particular. "Why's it still hot out?"

A shiver crept up Arthur's creaky spine.

No one answered Dumb Dick Rick. As one guard leant down to drink some water, another punched him in the groin with precision and speed. The man fell down in agony, immediately in a fetal position, clutching his assaulted balls. Laughter burst out of the other guards, the random act of cruelty on the same level as the finest stand-up comedian. Dumb Dick Rick, with a smile that revealed his rotten teeth, chest-bumped the attacker and shouted "Alpha male, dog! Alpha male!" Then he patted him on the back in affection.

The guard leaning on Arthur's cage spat out a giggle, and smoke poured out from underneath his mask.

Arthur looked on at his captors in disgust, at once not surprised by his own gender, but lacking any understanding in it. If Dewitt was right, if his experience in both worlds had proved a valid theory of man, was there any escaping this? Arthur knew that there was a life of casual violence and indifference to suffering ahead of him. If terrible things were going to happen to him, why not be defiant to it?

The man with the tattoos brought his arm up to show off the snakes to a different guard, but then he froze, looking bewildered. "Di-did my snake just move?" he said with an awe that sat neatly with fear and pleasure.

Arthur looked at the guard near him, the sheet metal armor reflecting what little light was left from the sun. *Fuck the consequences* he thought and moved toward Dewitt. He had questions, questions that his existential crisis demanded answers to, and tomorrow there was no guarantee he would be able to ask them. "Is there no future, sir? If we have always been like this, what can we do to break this cycle?"

Dewitt shuffled, then faced Arthur, his eyes tired and grey, looking as desperate as Arthur felt. "Who knows? Maybe nothing. Maybe we wait out this era of fallout and hatred and try again. Or maybe we just hand the reins to the women, and hope they don't castrate the lot of us."

"Good answer," said the guard in the sheet metal armor, more smoke pouring out of the helmet.

Rabia!

"Probably only castrate the worst of you demented swine and sell the festering genitalia off as power symbols to the other women in charge. So you two will be fine," Rabia whispered. "Also," she continued, "shut the fuck up, we're on break."

Arthur kept quiet. There was so much he wanted to say, and if there were no barriers between them (or madmen around them), he would have rushed in for a hug and squeezed like a bear. He would then apologize for being a headstrong zealot for a cause that did not share his affection. He would look into her burnt mahogany eyes, steal a glance at her beauty, and brace himself for the ugliest string of words he had ever heard.

The man holding his groin on the floor had rolled over, no longer doubled over in pain. He looked into the sky above, now dotted with a few stray stars and local planets. "It's so big," he said, "It's so fucking big". No one paid him any mind.

Dumb Dick Rick and the tattooed man were too busy gawking at the poorly drawn snakes, their jaws open in disbelief. "They *are* moving!" Dumb Dick Rick said.

The man in the tattoos screamed in terror. "GET THEM OFF! GET THEM OFF!"

Dumb Dick Rick grabbed the man's knife from out of his hands and hacked furiously at the tattooed arm.

Panic. Sheer bloody panic spread through the crowd of guards like a blighted thunderbolt.

"I put something in the water," Rabia said to Arthur, reaching into her pocket.

The sudden violence had stirred something in the guards that was not rational, and each dealt with it with flight or fight. There was laughter, tears, and raw animalistic screaming.

Rabia fished out a lock pick kit. She slid a long, L-shaped piece of metal into the padlock that was holding the door shut, then pulled out a crooked piece of metal and started to rake it towards her.

The guards around them paid them no attention. They were too busy either fighting each other or some invisible thing in the air that only they could see.

"What in god's name did you put in there?" Arthur asked.

"Everything," Rabia said as the padlock came undone. "I

put all of my drugs in there." The door swung open. "Well, except for the good feeling ones."

Dumb Dick Rick was now beating the man with the tattoos with his own severed arm. "It's not working!" he cried "The snakes are everywhere!"

Arthur crawled out of his cage as Rabia moved on to Dewitt's. She worked quickly on his padlock. "This deserves a raise," she said as the old man stumbled out of the cage. "A raise and a room."

"How did you...?" Dewitt tried.

"Easily," Rabia answered, "I'm a god damn professional!"

The two men followed Rabia, who was walking with urgency, but not running, through a path of cages. The men and women (and even a child) within the cages looked out to them in fear and desperation. Arthur met the eyes of each one he passed. *I will get you out,* he thought, *no matter what happens.*

The terrible cacophony of drugged-induced hysteria had reached a crescendo. Guards from all around had gathered to quell, or at least watch, the bedlam that had befallen their peers. Rabia shoved Arthur down behind an empty cage. Dewitt followed suit. Four guards, including the one with the rifle who had greeted them into this cruel hell, ran past them, too busy with the vicious circus ahead of them to notice the wounded bureaucrats being herded by a short, metal guard.

Rabia led Arthur and Dewitt inside the cage. Two more guards ran towards them, a mixture of pleasurable anticipation and fear on their faces. "Over there!" Rabia pointed to the trough. "One of them wants to fuck The Colonel!" she yelled. The moment they were gone, she led Arthur and Dewitt out of the cage.

Save for the endless rows of miserable people incarcerated in rusting boxes, the town was empty. They were soon at the far side of it, nearing a jumble of vehicles, all of them mutated into something horrible, and each capable of carrying at least one cage. "This is where they ship the slaves in and out," Rabia said, "We get in one of these junk demons while those Nazi cocksuckers are distracted and get the hell out of dodge!" She stopped suddenly and removed her helmet. Her kinky afro burst free from its constraints. Arthur's heart skipped a beat when she looked at him.

Rabia's heart did the same, but for an entirely different reason.

Before them was a rusted Chevrolet Impala convertible. Metal spikes were welded to the front of it and a large cage had taken root in the back seats. This Frankenstein of car and vicious junk had lost most of its red paint, but the large, manic smile of a shark had been painted on the hood of it. Rabia was immediately in love.

"We take this one," she said with awe. "Oh yes."

CHAPTER ELEVEN

At times it felt as though Rabia's driving was like trying to buck a Saturn Five rocket. Knuckle white tension and high octane fuel was the new law for the journey. Consequence could only ever happen if it caught up with you and, with their new ride, this was unlikely.

Truly, this was Rabia Duke, freelance Enforcer, at her best.

Arthur did not vomit, but only because there was no food in his system to purge.

Whether it was out of necessity, or minor revenge against 'the system', Commissioner Dewitt was seated inside the cage that was welded to the back of 'The Shark' (a name Rabia immediately adopted for the car, and enforced almost violently).

No one followed.

By the time the IRS agents had made it back to the van and drove it and The Shark to the horseshoe rock enclosure that Rabia and Arthur had camped out in the night before, a yellow-orange haze had engulfed Slaver City. The darkness of earth's own shadow had engulfed the valley and mountains, and the inhumane city they left behind had caught fire. Whatever calliope of drugged induced insanity they had left behind them, it had peaked with the wholesale destruction of at least three of the pre-war buildings.

Committing precious water to those buildings would be egregious. Instead, the denizens of Slaver City opted for the more abundant resource of sand, using every free and slave hand available to dig and snuff the fire out. As the fires faded, and much of the chaos had ceased, Rabia, Arthur and the Commissioner sat on top of a boulder, sharing provisions of food, water, and alcohol. They admired Rabia's professional handiwork.

Arthur finally accepted Rabia's offer of whiskey.

The three were in immensely good spirits. Watching the fire had done much for this, but freedom was surely the better opiate. Rabia lit a cigarette and slapped Arthur on the knee. "You are a real bastard," she said, affectionately. Her hand lingered. "You are lucky I'm a god damn professional."

Arthur took a swig of whiskey and then rebounded in horror as its hateful burn assaulted his throat, then numbed his senses. He wasn't quite drunk enough to reply to her with something cheesy like "I'm lucky to have you", but he did have enough courage to scoot closer to his knight in sheet metal, which, for Arthur, was about as suave as he was capable of. He passed the bottle to Dewitt, whose eyes had taken up a fire of their own after a couple of swigs, and no longer looked as tired as they had in his cage.

"How in the hell did you manage that?" Dewitt asked Rabia, passing back the bottle.

Rabia had her share of Wild Turkey, an amount that was alarming, and then turned to look at the old man. "Your employee of the year here had us caught in the 'spider's web', so to speak," she said, referring to Arthur as she slapped him on the back. "Once he was gone, I slit the throat of one of the guards as he came to drag me, and then shoved my 'Fly Swatter' to the other's dick before he could say anything. I threatened to kill him if he didn't give me his clothes..."

"And you used them as a disguise to sneak in?" Arthur asked intuitively.

"Christ no, he wouldn't hand them over, so I unzipped him with my knife from crotch to belly button," Rabia replied, removing her cigarette contemplatively. Both men stared at her in horror. Arthur moved away from her, just a little.

"I made my way back to the van, taking a different path than we came, had half the urge to drive back home too," she continued. "Spending a couple of days with this do-gooder was enough to guilt me back." She nodded at Arthur with a drunken smile. "So, I did what any God-fearing patriot would do, I packed my pockets with every high powered drug at my disposal and headed back with a cocktail of fear and loathing that would kill any lesser woman."

"*Then* you donned his armor and snuck inside?" Arthur tried again.

"Hell no, had to kill a different man for that. Came around on the backside of town nearest the cages and saw one of them pissing in a corner," Rabia answered, light-heartedly.

Dewitt raised his hand. "I don't need to know what you did to him," he said, half chuckling in fear.

Rabia shrugged. "Suit yourself."

"Tomorrow is going to be a big day," Dewitt said.

If Arthur was conflicted about how he felt about Rabia before, he wasn't now. Rabia was brave, or batshit insane, but however she wielded her traits, she did so admirably. Here was a woman who was truly in charge of herself. Oh, she was frightening, and her constant consumption of chemicals was worrying, but she was everything Arthur was not. She was commanding, decisive, and not bound to petty rules. She had somehow managed to do all of this in the United Wastes without losing her humanity or empathy. She had saved him, and he was man enough to admit that wasn't emasculating at all. Arthur had never been in love, but this felt like the start of it.

"We should leave early," Rabia said, "they should be too busy with damage control to send men out looking for us, but never underestimate the drive of revenge in a stupid man. We head home before dawn and we take both cars."

"We can't go home yet," Dewitt said. "We have a census to take."

Rabia's jaw dropped at this, and for a moment it looked as though her mind was not able to process what she had just heard.

"HAVE YOU LOST YOUR GOD DAMN MIND? Have worms been chewing on your amygdala? I just risked my god damn life to save you two *with* my personal medicine bag, something that I WILL bill you for, and you want to count heads?"

Dewitt nodded.

Rabia looked to Arthur for help.

"I agree. We have to go back," he said.

Dewitt looked at him approvingly. "You make the IRS proud."

Rabia looked as though a vein was about to burst in her head. Arthur could hear the distinct sound of grinding teeth and saw that the butt of her cigarette had been chewed down. She looked at Arthur, and the look of betrayal sunk his heart. He gathered his courage and realized he was likely going to disappoint both of them.

"We don't go back for the census though," Arthur finally managed. "We go back because there are people; helpless, innocent people, who are locked up in cages and have no future."

Rabia's eyes softened at this, and once more rested her hand on his knee. "You're a good man, Charlie Brown, but freeing those slaves is as suicidal as trying to get those cavemen Nazi bastards to fill out a census. We leave tomorrow."

"The hell we are!" Dewitt blurted, returning Rabia's anger. "I am not exactly happy about Boyd's trap, but we have a duty to fulfill and I am in charge goddammit!"

"THE HELL YOU ARE, YOU PENCIL DICKED BUREAUCRAT! I am a freelance Enforcer; I can terminate my contract whenever I want!" Rabia screamed, standing up and clutching the bottle of Wild Turkey like a throat. She looked down at Arthur pleading. "We would need an army to save those people, G-Man, and there is no pleasing *No*witt and Boyd."

"I think I know how to do both," Arthur said softly. He stood up, between Rabia and Dewitt. "Hear me out," he said.

"Whiskey is getting to your head G-Man," Rabia said, replacing her cigarette with a new one.

"No, maybe, well..." Arthur said, realizing that he had a slight slur. Dewitt rolled his eyes as Rabia sat back down. "The IRS has an army, one of the largest, and one The Colonel is afraid of. He thinks that the agency is going to raid him any day now, so there's no reason why he should be proven wrong."

Dewitt chuckled. "It isn't our department to free slaves or rescue the needy though, we collect taxes."

"Yes," Arthur replied, "and that is precisely what we are going to do. The Colonel has a record of every transaction that they make; he counted me in it before I was enslaved."

Dewitt's old eyes widened at this, and he vibrated with an

enthusiasm unknown to his withered bones in years. "That's genius!" he exclaimed.

"So?" Rabia said, "Who gives a fuck?"

Dewitt chimed in before Arthur had the chance. "We get that book, and the IRS will send out collection efforts en mass! If he's been keeping a record then we can try to collect back taxes!"

Arthur smiled. "The IRS has not been able to collect back taxes since The War. The Revised National Emergency Operations Guide forgives the back taxes of individuals. The Colonel's operation here is an entity large enough that can't be ignored and with that book to audit, we can seize his assets. And because those assets are people, his current inventory also counts as a census."

Smoke poured out from Rabia's lips and a look of terrible mischief lighted her face. "I get you two pencil-necked geeks. People are assets, and that book of his is the holy grail for the tax collector of the Armageddon era."

"You did it once before," Arthur said. "So will you help me sneak back in?"

Rabia took a long drag on her cigarette, then a long pull of whiskey. When that bottle was drained, she opened the tequila. "Why the hell not? No one should be a slave." She regarded Arthur with a warm smile then passed the tequila to Dewitt, who drank from it zealously. "Where is the book?" she asked.

"It's attached to the back of one of The Colonel's personal slaves," Arthur said with a mixture of anxiety, excitement and dread. This was likely suicide and the chances of them coming back from this were small, but his entire week had been filled with suicidal decisions, so what did one more matter? Either he was foolish or suicidal, but he wouldn't have to face which of these poisons of the mind had afflicted him most until after they succeeded or he was dead. "When I saw him, it looked like he was living under The Colonel's throne inside some ruble."

Dewitt nodded in agreement and then continued to drink the liquor. When Rabia looked at him with contempt, he passed it over to Arthur, his movement sluggish. "We do it in the morning," he said, with the beginnings of a slur softening his consonants. "An old man like me needs rest before he does something stupid," he continued before walking towards the van. "Good night."

Arthur and Rabia watched the ancient man saunter away. Once he was in the van, Arthur moved his attention back to Slaver City in the distance. The yellow-orange glow had dissipated and the glow of the moon had lit a pillar of black smoke. He could feel Rabia's warmth next to him.

Watching slavers die from a distance was so romantic.

"Give it to me straight, G-Man," she said, somber and serious. "Because this detail matters. Are you trying to do the right thing here, or is this a paper filing urge that you have to fill?" Her eyes spelled worry.

The pleading faces of men and women, beaten and bruised and forced into makeshift cages lined his mind. There was nothing he could have done that would not have put himself at risk, and he felt guilty for it. He had chosen, maybe wisely, maybe selfishly, to assure his own survival before their freedom. He had to do something about it. "It's better to die trying to do something that benefits others instead of a bureaucracy," he said, surprising himself. "The IRS can go to hell."

"I knew you were a shithead Boy Scout the minute I laid eyes on you," Rabia said, smiling ear to ear. "I knew you would probably get me killed, but what the hell? Buy the ticket take the ride." She took a swig of tequila, and then grabbed his hand. "You are a polite and kind person in a world of radioactive, insecure penises trying to fuck every-body over." She looked affectionately at him "It's refreshing."

Arthur wanted to draw her closer, but before he could, she grabbed his hand and abruptly jerked him to his feet. She let him go and fished for something in her pocket. Her hand came out closed, clutching something inside. Her wild eyes flashed with excitement. "Speaking of those racist, misogy-nistic Nazi swine bastards," she cursed, "remember I gave them all of the drugs *except* the good feeling ones." She opened her hand to reveal a bunch of capsules, which looked like a clutch of eggs held by a black, five tentacled squid. "What do you say, G-Man? We celebrate our freedom tonight, no rest for the wicked and no sympathy for the devil!"

Arthur regarded the capsules as if they were tiny pockets of fire. The little bit of alcohol he had drunk had already clouded his mind, but the call for carpe diem from a woman that had just saved his life was one he had to answer. He took a breath for courage and nodded his consent.

"Turn on, tune in, drop out," Rabia said, smiling prettily. She gave Arthur a single pill, then took three of them herself, washed down with tequila. She grabbed Arthur's hand once more.

Arthur looked at the single capsule tentatively. Then swal-lowed it.

CHAPTER TWELVE

Nothing happened for longer than Arthur was prepared for. The worst part was the anxiety he had, playing the waiting game. He thought perhaps a rabbit hole would open up beneath him, swallowing him whole and that he would be auditing hooka smoking caterpillars in a daze.

"Am I going to see something?" Arthur said, fear creeping into his voice.

"Sacrificed all of that stuff for those undeserving swine barbecuing below," Rabia replied, retrieving blankets, water and an ancient six-pack of beer from the van. "Not enough light to set up the tents," she said, laying the blankets on the ground, and then herself. She patted a space next to her, urging Arthur to join.

He did so, nervously.

"They don't make these anymore," Rabia said, cracking open a beer for herself, and then handing one over to Arthur. "I wasn't going to drink these for a while, but what the hell? We are probably going to die tomorrow anyways."

"You don't have to go," Arthur said.

"The hell I don't. We get that book and we can end some

suffering on a massive scale. That alone is worth the risk, plus someone needs to keep your dumb ass alive."

The drugs hit hard, and neurons in Arthur's brain fired off a 21 gun salute every half minute. The infinite span of stars shone brighter, and the endless void that they resided in became less monstrous and more wondrous. He was at once aware of how cold he was in the night's air and how vulnerable the earth he lay on was as it hurtled through space.

The feeling was good, but it was incredibly lonely.

His mind reeled back and forth in waves of ecstasy and helplessness, each one cresting higher than the other, and neither was more crushing than the hope he felt. He had been a caged man today. Caged as a slave to be sold, and caged in the routines and rigid structure of the IRS. It had occurred to him that at this moment, for the first time in his life, he was finally free.

The underground concrete hallways of the IRS bunker had been structured to keep him moving upwards in hierarchy, but always at the mercy of it. Freedom was not at the top of this ladder, as he had sorely learned sitting next to Dewitt in the slaver camp. He had said yes to everything that had ever come to him in paper form, while the planet around him whimpered its last breath. How much of his finite time had he traded counting other people's numbers for a note of currency from a dead era?

It wasn't until he was surrounded by a literal cage that it had occurred to him that he was never at the helm of his own life. Sure, a portion of that was mere survival, but that was a charge everyone in the United Wastes had to deal with; and still, there were those who found a way.

Euphoria weighed down on his body, and the 21 gun salute firing off neurons in his brain had become a constant, rapid fire of buckshot.

It was just him and the lonely, far away, dead stars. He

shivered from the cold, even though he was wrapped in a blanket. He was suddenly fully aware of every detail of his tactile senses and found the chill impossible to ignore.

Rabia pressed her warm body against his, which took the nip out of his chill and displaced his sense of being utterly alone.

Rabia.

Somehow free, self-destructive, mad even, but she had retained her humanity. It was hard for him to imagine how he had ever resented her.

He wanted to say everything that was on his mind, the infinite universe, his self-built cage, how much he admired her and how god damn thankful he was. It was hard to push through the drugs to speak, but he had finally found his voice, and once he'd started...

Rabia was straddling him. "Once we get talking with this high powered beast, neither of us is going to want to stop," she said, her warm body pressed against his. "We might not make it past tomorrow, so why don't we save the chit-chat and break some office rules?" There was no thinking here, there was no need to. Arthur reached up and kissed her.

Then with devilish urgency, they shed clothes.

His heart raced. Her skin was soft and warm, her kiss deep and voracious. He could feel her hips pressing greedily on his own...

...But nothing was happening.

Her eyes were still placid with the endorphin rush of the drug, but a tinge of frustrated disappointment was there. She let out a sigh. "You're not going to get hard, are you?"

The question made Arthur bashful, ashamed. He was not able to spit out more than "I uh, I don't, ah..."

"Don't worry about it," Rabia said, climbing off. "That's probably the A in the MDMA, it happens. We'll do the dirty when we are sober."

This didn't do much to assure him, or calm his feelings of being inadequate. Sensing this, she teased, "*if* we live long enough, but you know, whatever." She took a long pull of beer, and then cuddled into him, resting her head on his chest.

"I'm sorry," he said, as every ounce of him except his penis was up for the dirty deed.

"Please be man enough to not make me console your ego right now," Rabia said. "Besides, this," she said, cuddling up tighter "is not overrated".

He held her naked body tight to his own. She was right.

"I'm sorry," he said once more.

"What the hell did I just say, Arthur?" Rabia snapped.

"No, not for that, I'm sorry for today. I'm sorry that we have to go back. I'm sorry for everything."

The waves of euphoria he had felt were now coming in as big combers. The joy of tactile touch and the glitter of stars were overwhelming for a moment but he soon hungered for more.

He was powerless in the face of the monolithic paper shoveling at the IRS. It was the last place on the planet where civility remained, where human decency was a luxury not yet snuffed out by the savagery of the United Wastes. But it still robbed a human of their significance, reducing them to something that could be thrown away. He was reduced, his power as an intelligent being marginalized, he was just a number: A-24.

His mind was easily distracted. Rabbit holes of thoughts could be followed with such ease. He felt Rabia's weight on him, her breath, and her heart beat. He could feel her wool-like hair on his shoulder. Gravity was suddenly so oppressive. Life was so absurd. His mind was easily distracted.

How much time had he spent on this planet? How much time had been wasted? A lot. That was proper, living in the

United Wastes and all. He had been here longer than his father. He had become his father, hadn't he? Gone on the same suicidal quest for reasons that only made sense when you were sober. Fuck being sober.

"Did you say something?" Rabia asked.

He had. He had said something he felt so powerfully, but what was it? How long ago was that? How long had it been since she asked him if he had said anything? Was that a moment ago? She's so soft. How could she be so soft on the outside but be so hard on the outside? Wait. Was that right? It had to be. She was so much braver, but that was good news, wasn't it? If she was braver than he was brave. He was brave. Brave or stupid. Probably stupid. He felt sorry.

!!!!

"I said I'm sorry about tomorrow, I think. I'm sorry I can't let those people suffer."

"Don't be. Don't ever feel sorry about that, G-Man. One of us damned souls has to have a conscience. Sometimes I feel like mine burnt out a long time ago. It's good to have you here to remind me that I still care. For some reason, I still care."

The drug receded, for a moment. Rabia didn't feel so heavy, gravity suddenly felt trivial. Her words were powerful, like they could be sigils. They had power because they were true. His feet were cold. He wanted to kiss her, to try and see if he could make something happen, but the drug crested and rolled down on top of him again, and the energy needed to move felt impossible. He was content to just pass his hands across her thighs. He felt many scars and wondered if she regretted that they were permanent. She still cared. She had still, somehow, managed to keep a degree of humanity, even though she had murdered two people today.

She moved her fingers across his chest greedily, and then sighed deeply.

"I wish I didn't get rid of the acid," she said. "It's not nearly as fucking cheesy as this."

CHAPTER THIRTEEN

The quickest way from one place to another is a straight line, but quick did not meet the demands of the insane.

The van roared through the United Wastes near a pace that might shake it apart, its engine screamed in agony. There was no letting up. Hell was going to be kicked in the groin.

Clouds of dust and frightened exhaust pumped out from beneath the van, leaving behind a large tail of toxic grief.

It was not built for this speed. Something had to give.

Nothing did.

It could be spotted from miles away. The guards fired shots into the air, notifying the others that they were under siege.

No one comes at them this fast to talk. It was all hands on deck.

Some of them were bruised, some of them were burnt. All of them were tired.

The rancid, drug-fueled anarchy that reigned supreme the night before, ending in a crescendo of fire and agony had left them weak, suspicious, and stupid. Still, they were The

Colonel's men, and whatever came howling at them now was far less terrifying than the tyrant with the wattle.

They wanted revenge.

And so, every man whose mind was ravaged by a cocktail of vicious, high powered chemicals, and every man that was ravaged by those men, needed to see the van die.

When it was close enough for the guards to notice, it was too late.

The van was on fire.

Impotent shots rang out of rifles, pistols, and the occasional handmade weapon, but the momentum was too strong. Only God himself could slow this white IRS beast down, and God left the premises when the first bomb fell.

Nothing was certain but death and taxes. These two things are not exclusive.

The van exploded forward, easily making it past the four-lane wide gate, and careened into the makeshift city hatefully, never once deviating from its straight line.

Screams of terror were washed out by screams of rage. The slavers were having none of this.

The van rammed into the side of an old concrete building, once used for banking, now used for dog slaughter.

Nothing would have survived that crash.

The guards stepped towards it tentatively.

CHAPTER FOURTEEN

The IRS always knocked on your front door, but this is Armageddon. While the front was on fire, they snuck in from the back door.

"Do all of your plans involve violent distractions?" Arthur asked Rabia.

"As often as god damn possible. Refuge in audacity," she replied, getting out of The Shark, but leaving it running.

The large boulder they had placed on the van's gas pedal had done its work beautifully, but they got the sense it would be the only agent to stay in one piece.

There was no shortage of guns between them. Rabia carried her red shotgun, a machete at her back, and an obscenely large hand cannon with a scope that would look comical had she not had the cold stare emanating from her tired face. Dewitt grabbed a rifle from her weapon cache and met no protests. Rabia handed Arthur a small pistol. "After how you handled your own last night, I don't really trust you with one of these," she teased, looking at him affectionately. "Don't get yourself killed."

Dewitt and Arthur led the way, feverishly familiar with the city by their water carrying path.

Arthur was burnt out. The potency of the drug had kept him from the release of sleep, and when it had finally weaned, Rabia insisted on pumping Bob Dylan and Jefferson Airplane into the night. He had no idea how she was as ornery as she was today. The crazy bitch never seemed to sleep, and even now, despite being low on drugs, she raced forward without looking back. Her constitution was a gift from the gods, or a sordid deal with the devil. Neither would have surprised him.

They had decided to raid in the morning when the slavers were still cradling their wounds, but why they had decided to do this hungover and burnt out from MDMA was anyone's guess. If that was the good feeling drug, Arthur could not imagine what hell the guards were going through.

They moved quickly and quietly towards The Colonel's roost, but they were only halfway there when a guard yelled out "THERE IS NO ONE INSIDE THE VAN!" So they picked up the pace, clinging to the walls as much as possible. It was only a matter of time before the guards fanned out.

The Terror Throne was just blocks away, a tiny beacon for their journey. The Colonel was not there, so they honed in on it.

The angry yells of pissed off guards grew closer.

Dewitt's age was deceptive to how quickly he could move, but getting him to start was a chore. He held his rifle firm and close, the tip aimed low at all times. It had never occurred to Arthur that he fought in The War before it became an atomic theater, but seeing him now, it was easy to imagine a younger commissioner storming the beaches of a foreign land. Dewitt hugged a wall then peeked out to the side, seeing the old fast food restaurant ahead of them. "We run across one at a time," he said, "when we are all there, we breach."

Arthur clicked his pen.

Dewitt charged across then hugged the restaurant's wall nearest to the window that the emaciated man had climbed out of the day before. He looked out from his spot then signaled that it was clear.

Arthur ran next. Then Rabia.

The shouting drew nearer.

They could see nothing inside from the window, save the bright primary colors of a counter. One by one, they climbed inside.

The interior of the restaurant was mostly empty, the cash register, the gaudy furniture and even most of the kitchen equipment had been pulled out of it, likely scavenged years ago. The little light that there was illuminated thick motes of dust. Only half of the restaurant was intact, the other half caved in, now the makeshift home of The Colonel on top. The centerpiece to this old fast-food dining area was the emaciated man, riddled with tumors, the large book still strapped to his back. He was holding an old, half melted doll and a pink plastic toy brush. His eyes widened, and he clutched the doll close to his chest.

"Hand it over, we are federal agents—" Dewitt started before the screaming began.

"Noooo!" The emaciated man screeched. "You can't have it!"

The three were conscious of how close the guards were. This screaming was not helping.

"Listen up you creepy fuck!" Rabia said through her teeth. "You are gonna hand over what we want or you'll find your teeth splattered on that god damn wall!"

"No! You can't take her!" the man wailed, clutching the doll closer.

"What? No, um sorry," Arthur said. "We want the book, not the doll. Um, give us the book, okay?"

"Oh," the emaciated man said, his sobs shortening, "you can have the book. I hate this book, it's really heavy." And with that, he unstrapped the belts.

Some of the guards could now be heard around the restaurant, but thankfully did not come in. The sound of heavy footsteps drummed on the collapsed ceiling.

"He's here," the emaciated man whispered. "Be quiet, he doesn't know that I have her, he'll be furious," he continued, handing the oversized book to Dewitt.

They were surrounded.

Moving like a lithe express train, Rabia was within inches of the emaciated man in a breath. She pressed her shotgun firmly against the doll and looked over her aviators directly into the man's eyes. "Go outside and lead those swine away from us or the doll gets a hole in its chest large enough to stick your fist through," she whispered.

"Rabia, you can't solve all of your problems with a diversion," Arthur said.

"The hell I can't!" Rabia responded with no love in her eyes. "We start drawing gunfire now and we'll be surrounded before we get anywhere close to The Shark." She turned her attention back to the emaciated man, clutching the doll to his heart. "Do you know what a triple-aught buckshot can do to plastic?"

"I'll do it I'll do it, just don't hurt her!" he said, wild desperation in his eyes. He lowered the doll slowly to the ground and stepped away from it.

"Arthur, get that strapped to your back, we leave on my signal," Rabia ordered. Dewitt held the book to Arthur's back and the two of them worked to get the leather tongue like latches around him. When it was secured, Rabia, with her red shotgun, motioned to the emaciated man to leave from a window.

The agents gathered together near an opposite window.

Arthur and Dewitt tentatively awaited Rabia's command and their chance to flee. The emaciated man climbed out of the same window they had come in and then immediately screamed for help. "There's a bad woman down there!" he shouted "a very bad woman!" The silence that followed was suffocating, and then shuffling feet broke it as guards raced towards the old diner.

Steps hammered above them, drowned out by the booming voice of The Colonel. "Bring me her head so that I may fuck it!"

"We should go now," Rabia said, and then she jumped out of the window.

As soon as they were all out, they ran as fast as they could, legs pumping furiously.

The first guard they saw held a tire iron in his one and only hand. Buckshot erupted from Rabia's shotgun and the tire iron fell to the ground before the body followed. Arthur could hear the bitter spray of bullets from Dewitt's rifle, but he couldn't see their target. He ran without thinking. Soon they were at the corner across from The Colonel's roost and Arthur dared to look behind him. The Colonel was on his throne, his wattle wagging back and forth. "It's the IRS!" he bellowed, pointing his sausage finger at Arthur. "Bring me their heads and I'll share one!"

Arthur was jerked forward. Rabia had grabbed him by the tie, yanking him back into momentum. *We are going to die,* he thought, but followed her as fast as his shoes could kick the ground.

Dewitt turned a corner and was out of sight for a split second. Arthur heard the sharp crack of gunfire and when he turned the corner himself saw a guard clutching his bleeding belly with both hands. They continued to run.

The sound of heavy footsteps thundered behind them.

The further Arthur jammed forward, the closer they seemed to be.

Another corner turned and four guards stood at the ready, each clutching a different firearm. Rabia reeled back and pushed the boys in a different direction. Their cover of old prewar buildings was thinning. Soon they would be in the field of cages, which would present a whole new set of challenges. With Rabia pushing them forward, Arthur was now in the lead. Dewitt began to slow.

Arthur ran to the edge of another building and turned the corner.

A guard greeted him on the other side. His jagged, rotten, fang-like teeth showed from behind an open gash of a mouth. He pointed his rifle directly at Arthur.

Guns go up? Don't frown! Fall down!

As he fell backward, Arthur raised his pistol and squeezed off half a dozen bullets.

To his surprise, one hit the man in the shoulder causing him to shriek with pain. Before he could retaliate, Rabia had turned the corner and shot off a round. The guard's jaw exploded into stains of blood and teeth around him, giving Jackson Pollock a run for his money.

The weight of the book, and its large flat surface prevented Arthur from rolling over. He was like a turtle, vulnerable and belly up towards any birds of prey sharp enough to spot a kill. They were in a narrow alleyway, the decaying walls of old buildings squeezing them in. Dewitt had joined them, a grim look on his face. The old man let his rifle fall to his side, caught by a shoulder strap, and offered his hands to his subordinate.

Arthur was pulled up to the sound of gunfire. Dewitt fell to the ground.

A guard had caught up from behind.

Rabia fired three shots into his chest and he fell to the ground, next to the man he'd just killed in cold blood.

Arthur clicked his pen, expecting form 22-B *Violent Incident in the Workplace* to be on his phantom clipboard.

Blood had swelled out of Dewitt's back, mixing with dirt to form a grim mud. Rabia's cries to move on faded into the background. Arthur was witnessing the death of the highest IRS official he had ever had the pleasure to meet. Dewitt's wrinkled hands drew Arthur close. "Leave, I'm old, we must audit this place; get the book home," and with a labored breath, added "please, file an HR complaint against Boyd for me."

Tears welled in Arthur's eyes, threatening to consume his sight. The sounds of frantic footsteps grew louder and louder.

"I'm sorry, sir," Arthur said, "but I'm an Auditor, that's just not my department."

A smile fanned across the old man's face for the last time, "That-a-boy," Dewitt said with understanding. Then, he had the decency to die.

Rabia spun Arthur about-face, terror dominating her eyes. "Get moving you dirty bastard!" she said.

The pain of a side stitch and lactic acid threatened to slow him, but still he ran. He followed Rabia as the sound of hurried feet clamored behind them.

They were in the field of cages.

Arthur hoped that the guards would not dare fire off shots at them here, that they would not want to risk damaging their 'products', but the contrary was immediately confirmed. Shots rang past Arthur and the slaves around him fell to the floors of their cages in cover.

They weaved between the cages, doing their best to confuse their pursuers and avoid being shot.

Arthur had an irrational fear that turning around to see

how many slavers were in pursuit would somehow bring them closer. They passed his former cage. His legs threatened to shut down. The book behind him weighed on his aching spine. He was dizzy with pain.

But there was no choice but to sprint.

They had cleared the field and were met with the grisly rusted mutant car fleet. The worst feeling in the world had managed to bloom in Arthur's mind: hope.

Rabia rocketed towards The Shark, its engine still pumping out toxic fumes. That's when they saw him. On the hood of the car was Dumb Dick Rick, a cruel smile on his stupid face and a giant shotgun in both his hands. "Lookie here, the pretty black—"

But before Dumb Dick Rick could finish his sentence, Rabia fired two shots, and then Rick had no Dick.

Dumb Rick fell forward and writhed on the ground like a live wire. Rabia booted him in his bloody groin, just for good measure.

"Don't you ever wink at me again, you dumb Nazi fuck!" she yelled, and then promptly got in the car.

As soon as Arthur joined her, she slammed down on the accelerator. Arthur lurched forward, scrambling to unlatch the book so he could put on his seat belt (old habits). They sped backward, wheels screeching, as Arthur managed to remove the book.

There was a single solitary bullet hole in the front of the thick tome.

Arthur opened its pages and found that the bullet had tunneled to a stop at the back cover.

When he looked up, he saw about a dozen slavers, half of them firing madly, the others scrambling to mount mutant cars of their own.

His view quickly changed as Rabia turned the steering

wheel. She switched gears and they roared forward. Arthur clutched the book to his chest at the same time securing his seat belt.

Engines roared. Rabia smiled.

CHAPTER FIFTEEN

Up a god damn mountain, that's where they had to be. It was a tall order, and not just because of the 6000 feet in elevation they had to climb; first they had to survive long enough to get to the base of it.

The Shark jettisoned them forward with erratic force. It had taken them all morning to walk from the base of the mountain to Slaver City the day before, but at the breakneck gonzo crazy speed that Rabia was driving they would likely get there before the hour was done.

An hour is an eternity when you are being chased by testosterone-fueled maniacs, especially when the words 'consent' and 'empathy' are as foreign to them as the Kuiper Belt.

No matter how much distance they made from Slaver City, they couldn't widen the gap between them and the psychopaths behind them.

Truly, things that were far worse than death were only an error away from descending on them with a rabid fury that would make the berserkers of old blush.

Arthur was filling out paperwork.

It was probably not the best thing that he could be doing

with his time, seeing as there were a dozen men behind them that wanted to turn his skull into a sex toy, but what else was he supposed to do? He could barely fire a gun at a stationary person only a few yards away, there was no way he could get a shot off on a moving vehicle going at a rate with no regard to safety. He had a 22-B *Violent Incident in the Workplace* form to fill out, and he had time to do it.

Rabia was inventing new ways to curse at their socio-pathic pursuers.

"You festering shit-buckets!" She yelled behind her.

Name of employee or victim of the violent incident: Jack Dewitt.

The cars behind them had closed some distance. The old Shark's muscle engine, built in the 1970s, was just not able to outperform the newer models.

"You black-hearted used car salesmen Nazi fucktards, I hope you choke on your red pills!" Rabia spat.

Position/Grade of employee/victim: Commissioner of Operations. The labor of a high-speed chase made the cars behind them whine.

"Pus cunt! PUS. CUNT!" Rabia screamed.

Events leading up to the violent incident as seen by the filler of this form:

"DID YOU HEAR ME, YOU BASTARDS?!"

Arthur looked up at Rabia, the woman that had stolen his heart, with a look of terror. "That one was horrible," he said. She smiled mischievous, smoke pouring out her nostrils like a dragon.

"You killed a man today and witnessed terrible apprehensible violence, yet that word is where you draw the line?" she nipped, gripping the steering wheel as if it were a neck she was trying to strangle.

"*You* killed that man; I could barely hit him in the shoulder!" Arthur retorted. Silence rolled out to a length that was uncomfortable.

"Thank you, by the way, that's the second time you saved me," Arthur said, breaking it.

The screams of raw vocal chords could be heard over the agonized purr of engines.

The slavers were closing the distance. "I'm still saving you!" Rabia said, glancing at him and clocking his clipboard. Her eyes widened. "IS THIS REALLY THE BEST TIME FOR THAT?"

Arthur considered her question. He looked in the rearview mirror and saw a gang of slavers. They were still too far away to shoot, but even in the short time he looked at them, they had got bigger. Arthur's finite life, in just a moment, could be measured rather than guessed.

"Yes," he replied, after considering that form 22-B was 40 lines long.

The mountain ahead of them looked no bigger. It was no guarantee of safety and was an ample reminder of how long they had been chased. What was the plan once they were climbing it? What would happen if they were never able to gain any distance, and their pursuers followed them all the way back to the IRS bunker? The IRS snipers surrounding their borders could drop a few *if they were on foot*, but the rest?

They had transferred their supplies from the van to The Shark, most tightly packed away in the back and some in the steel cage behind them. Seeing that they were in a convertible, it was conceivable that Arthur could climb over and grab whatever they needed, allowing Rabia to continue driving like a drowning bitch, but were they mentally prepared for the long haul? Having dogs biting at your heels for that long was mentally and emotionally exhausting.

Maybe I should wait to finish this form, Arthur thought. *It might give me something to do when the adrenaline is permanently spent and we still have days to go.*

Days to go might be a little too optimistic.

The slavers started firing.

"Son of two whores!" Rabia spat as more shots fired. "Unholster my hand cannon and take a crack at them; and for god sakes, man, try and hit something!"

As Arthur unclipped the top of her holster, he noticed the tendons in her legs were tense like taut ropes as she kept the pedal to the floor. He unbuckled his seatbelt and turned round.

"Pick the bastard you want dead, look down the scope of that monster, and unleash hell," Rabia demanded.

No longer did Arthur want to be the burden to protect. Too many Enforcers had lost their lives and Rabia's was one that he wanted to preserve. He pointed the gun at an old Volkswagen with oversized tires twice the size than what was reasonable and a collection of buzzsaws for a fender. He looked down the scope and sighted a slaver.

Unleash hell.

He pulled the trigger... The recoil startled him so completely that he dropped the gun outside of the car, and to add insult to injury, he missed his target.

"Why are you so fucking useless with phallic symbols?" Rabia yelled, her voice slightly fried from the punishment of anger she had flooded into it. "Do I have to do everything?" She snapped her fingers. "Alright, I've got a plan. Glove compartment, hand me one of my...treats."

Embarrassed and ashamed, Arthur opened the glovebox expecting to find drugs or alcohol, but instead he found four metal pipes capped off on each side. He took one out and found that the end facing away carried a fuse. Pipe bombs.

The blunted sound of a bullet rang off of the back side of The Shark.

Arthur's nerves had cracked. The sound of the bullet connecting had sent him down and behind his seat like a turtle receding into their shell. He handed the pipe bomb to Rabia. "Is this another distraction?"

Rabia looked at him wickedly. She held the steering wheel in place with her knees, lit the fuse with her cigarette and chucked the pipe bomb out the window hatefully. "Explosions are distracting," she said, sweetly.

It bounced twice on the ancient and beaten pavement before exploding, concussive force and shrapnel tearing and mangling everything near it. All that was left of the Volkswagen and its occupants: modern art.

Rabia cackled. "Take that you god damn swine!" she yelled.

Clearly concerned they might meet the same fate, the cars behind them slammed on the brakes.

"I built these the last time I was paid by the IRS," Rabia said, casually. "So, technically this is our tax-paying dollars hard at work." She motioned for another one. "Keep an eye on them; if they get close again we can toss another."

Arthur handed her another pipe then turned around. They had given them distance, but much of the slaver fleet had caught up with the others. Four Harley Davidson motorcycles, chained together like sled dogs, made their way to the front. From what Arthur understood of the beasts they might have been the only vehicles in the mutant fleet that were heavily modified *before* The War. These bikes, and their riders, were the apocalyptic equivalent of Huns on horseback. Arthur did a double take, taking a moment to register the madness he was witnessing. If the Harley Davidsons were sled dogs, the sled was a familiar grim throne made of teeth and bullets, fashioned into a chariot.

The Colonel.

His hideous wattle blew in the wind.

One of the riders pulled a sawed-off shotgun from his back, holding the pistol grip tightly, and fired at them.

Arthur ducked as hot buckshot licked his earlobe.

"Now!" he yelled, cowering behind his seat.

The pipe bomb flew directly into the path of The Colonel's chariot, but one of the riders was quick off the mark, disconnected from the others, pulled ahead and intercepted it. The bomb ripped him and his metal stead to shreds, painting the pavement with blood. Unaffected by the carnage, The Colonel raged forward.

Arthur desperately wanted to return to his paperwork. He was clicking his pen in a rapid-fire succession. Arthur met Rabia's eyes in the rearview mirror as she gave The Colonel the bird.

The mountain looked to be only slightly closer.

"Will a bomb be enough to stop that thing?" Arthur asked, unable to hide his fear.

"Don't know," Rabia said then held out her hand. A smile crept onto her face. Arthur handed her the third bomb, leaving one left.

Another knee on the wheel, another puff of smoke and the pipe was on its maiden voyage.

Another rider detached and drove towards it, a guttural yell erupting from him. The pipe bounced off of the motorcycle and then splattered it on the road as it exploded.

The Colonel had to swerve only slightly. He was not going to let up, and the loss of two of his sled dogs did nothing to deter him.

"God damn it!" Rabia screamed. "I wanted to set these off to celebrate once we got home. This is a waste of my talent!"

Arthur removed the final pipe from the glove compartment with unease. He thought about praying but was certain that whatever god was left to hear him needed none of this and that praying for a bomb to hit its mark was a decidedly terrible thing to petition a higher power for. Instead, he clicked his pen twice. "You know," he said, "this is technically work supplies for you, I can help you get this deducted from this year's taxes."

"Stop flirting," Rabia replied to a man who was completely serious "and put that away for now. They have no idea how many of these things we have; let them think we ran out. Take some shots at him instead but don't drop my god damn gun, G-Man." The Colonel had backed off a bit, probably anticipating another of Rabia's 'arts and crafts' to come tumbling towards him. Still, he was close enough that Arthur could see his rancid chin flap.

Arthur pulled out his pistol Rabia gave him earlier.

Arthur knew he couldn't shoot a gun to literally save himself. He knew that he would likely miss and just end up making a lot of noise. He knew it would probably be another exercise in failing to do something that was considered masculine and hoping that his companion would not give him too much shit for it. But that wattle! It would be worth it if he could just shoot that ugly thing.

Arthur laid his gun over the top of his seat, using it to steady his hand. He lined up his sight, took a deep breath, exhaled, and pulled the trigger.

In a universe of chaos and indifference where the absolute worst that can happen does, and without fail, in a world of devastation and atomic annihilation, good things occasionally peek their heads above the parapet. It is these small, often deserved moments that make life worth living. Despite the colossal amount of shit that the universe can fling at you, random chance is sometimes on your side. Sometimes the meek get what is owed to them.

This was decidedly not one of those moments.

Arthur not only missed, but The Shark hit a rough patch of road, projecting the pistol from Arthur's hand out of the window and into oblivion..

...and Rabia had seen *everything*.

"Sorry," Arthur said, embarrassed. He sunk into his seat and fastened his seatbelt to its locked position. Arthur looked directly ahead, doing his best not to meet Rabia's eyes.

"I'm really sorry." Arthur tried, easing the situation, not at all.

Rabia drew a knife and with a quick jerking motion, cut through Arthur's seatbelt.

"Under no circumstances do you get another gun," Rabia spat. "How in god's name are you the only man in the entire godforsaken United Wastes who can't fire a gun? How have you survived this long?"

Not knowing which to answer first, and suspecting he was on a two-word basis with her, he said "Don't know," then continued to look forward, clicking his pen again.

The mountain had finally graced most of the horizon and the dead, skeleton-like trees that lined it and its base were near. Soon they would be back in a forest of hard, dry wood.

"Hand over your shoe," Rabia said, puffing on a cigarette and no longer looking angry.

"What? No. Why?"

Like a rock hitting still water, Rabia's face turned from serene to uncorked anger. "You lost your god damn shoe privilege when you lost *two* of my favorite guns. Did you see how god damn shiny they were? It was obscene how much time I spent polishing them Arthur, *fucking obscene*. Now you hand over your shoe so that I can throw it at these god damn animals!" The shoe was off his foot and in her hands in a moment. He had no want for Rabia's rage, and besides not having a proper toolkit for conflict resolution (save for passively aggressively filing papers to HR), the shoe allowed for equilibrium. If all that those two guns would cost him was a shoe, well, that was a trade he would make.

"Now hand me the pipe," she said.

They had passed the first few trees, and were soon

surrounded by them. Each desolate spire made way for a thicker piece of forest and the deeper they drove, the closer to the road the trees became..

Rabia threw the shoe overboard.

The Colonel gave it a wide berth as if it were another pipe bomb. Not willing to sacrifice themselves, the remaining motorcyclists came to a halt.

It took The Colonel a few seconds to realize what had happened. He fired a shot in the air then commanded his riders to move on forward again. The chariot was slow to accelerate, and was becoming a point on the horizon.

Rabia cackled with delight. They pushed on and made good distance. Arthur let out a relieved laugh.

We are going to make it, Arthur thought to himself, *that witty sexy maniac bought us some space and we are going to make it.*

Rabia threw the last pipe bomb lit and with a panicked fuse at the foot of a tree. The base exploded in a cloud of splinters and the ancient dead thing fell over into the road.

It was magnificent.

It then promptly lit the surrounding dead forest on fire.

CHAPTER SIXTEEN

Well-earned relief did not find the two for some time. There was simply no room for it. The felled tree was enough to stymie The Colonel and the forest fire would keep him at bay. Away from their pursuers, and with the book they could use to bring freedom to many, they now had to escape an enemy far worse because it was destructive with indifference: the fire.

This was not an immediate concern, as at first it seemed as though The Shark would rally far ahead of it, leaving it as distant smoke on the horizon. But this forest, filled with the bones of trees, was dryer than the surface of mercury. It might as well have been an ocean of kindling because the effect was the same. The fire spread from one tree to the next in a flash, moving in every direction. Only ten minutes had gone since they set it and the air was already thick with oppressive smoke. Then minutes more and ashes would fall like snow. Once they were at the top of the mountain, near where they had set up camp for the past two days, the fire had caught up to them. It had no need to follow the road like they had and it spread furiously. The skeletal spires that covered the mountain blazed in a hellish inferno. It had become a place Satan himself could easily call home, or at least a place that would make a killer image for a heavy metal album.

Had there been any life in the old grove of dead trees, animals would flee in desperate droves, but man had taken care of them a generation ago. With his adrenaline spent and his nerves raw and tired, Arthur took the inferno that raged around him with a surreal sort of stride. *This is no tragedy*, he thought as Rabia navigated the mountain's windy road, *a forest is something that is alive, maybe this is just tidying up the mountain.*

If it was being tidied, it was being done *feverishly*. The road descended in a zigzag. They were prisoners to the whims of the road, but the fire was not. It looked like the fire was going to overtake them on their right.

The smell of smoke burned their nostrils, and the light around them had taken on an almost urine like quality; urine from a person with dehydration. The Shark gave them no shelter from it and the toxic air easily made its way into the cabin.

Rabia, of course, was still smoking cigarettes. This was stressful, after all.

If God had wanted them to die, then he blinked and lost his place. The fire went in the direction *it* wanted to and was more content to take out the rest of the forest laterally, instead of moving downward. For now anyway. The road's corners were tight. Arthur felt nauseous and Rabia looked exhausted. After an hour's drive, they had made it back to the base of the mountain, leaving hell behind them.

After driving a mile from the mountain's base, Rabia slowed to a stop. Her knuckles eased from the steering wheel. She sighed deeply, releasing some tension and stress. He reached for his seatbelt buckle (forgetting that Rabia had lobbed it off), then got out the car, half fearing the onset of another crisis. Instead, he found Rabia by his side with two beers and a weary smile. They cheered their libations and drank up, gazing at the burning mountain behind them.

"Staring at massive fires we have caused can totally be our thing," Rabia said, "it is super romantic."

Arthur watched the nightmarish scene unfold, not feeling it to be the least bit romantic. But before he could say anything, Rabia pulled softly on his tie and drew him in for a kiss. Her lips were chapped, the air around them was thick with smoke and the taste of cigarettes on her tongue wasn't particularly appealing, but he embraced her tightly, and his heart sang.

She was right. This was somehow romantic, in a demented, twisted, and gonzo-crazy way, but just the same. They leaned on the hood of the car and swigged their beers. For the first time, the silence that fell between them was not awkward, it was an understanding. Someday, when the fire had eaten all of the wood, they would be back here, and when that happened they would have an army with them.

"I feel like we just stole the plans to the Death Star," Arthur said with a chuckle.

"What in the hell is that?" Rabia asked, a single eyebrow poking above her shades.

"It's from a movie they show in the bunker every Christmas," Arthur replied, now nostalgic for his concrete cubicle and homesick for paperwork. "It's about a farmer and space wizards."

"Indeed."

"It makes more sense when you see it."

With a final, long pull, Rabia emptied her bottle and threw it on the pavement ahead of them, shattering it into dozens of pieces. Arthur was getting used to her sudden bursts of aggression, so he decided to launch his bottle too.

Rabia looked up at Arthur, passed a second beer to him

and lit another cigarette. "What happens now, G-Man? We got your book; was it worth losing some top brass and government property?"

"I don't know," Arthur replied honestly. "With Dewitt dead, that means Boyd has him out the way, like he wanted. The IRS will follow its letter though; those people will be liberated when we collect back taxes. Maybe making the world a little bit less cruel was worth it." He looked at the ground, burdened by recent memories, then glanced up at Rabia. "Hmm, maybe not."

"To hell with that," Rabia said with conviction. "Your goody-two-shoe bullshit is starting to rub off on me, G-Man, but before I met you I didn't think the world could be less cruel. We did good today *and* we taught those Nazi bastards something they will never forget: don't fuck with us."

Arthur contemplated this and relented that they had at the very least achieved the latter. The mountain behind them was testament to it. He started to run the consequences of their journey in his mind and came to a likely path it would lead to. Boyd would be in charge, and it was clear that he was hungry for power, so surely he would take the book as a trophy for his census campaign. Arthur would come home to no promotion and would have to answer to Ralph. Safety had not found him, the thing that he had coveted the most, and the thing he was promised was no longer possible.

But was that so bad? He would be auditing by Rabia's side and he couldn't think of a person he would rather spend hell with. After what they had just done, what was some more audit work in the United Wastes? Further, an institution of slavery was in the crosshairs of the same organization that brought down the mob in the 1930s. Arthur had lost sight of his office dreams, but he had gained a friend and disillusion- ment from his hero. That last part was bitter, and though he might have been happier staying in ignorance, he would not have grown.

Arthur wrapped his arm behind Rabia's back and drew the side of her hips to his. She moved her hand up his back, and they drank their beers in a companionable silence. The thing that no one tells you about forest fires is that they produce *the best* sunsets. As the sun slowly dipped toward the horizon, red-streaked like blood on a purple carpet in the sky, the yellow-orange haze of the inferno lit up the mountain. If Arthur's adrenal gland could keep up with the abuse, he very much would have loved to spend his life with Rabia.

"Don't break my heart, G-Man," Rabia said, "or I'll shove an icepick behind your eyes and scramble your frontal lobe."

"You're horrifying," Arthur retorted. "Also after what I've seen you do," he pointed at the mountain with his beer, "if I break your heart, I'm going to eat a bullet before you can get to me."

"Good deal," said Rabia. She took a long pull off of her beer, tossed the bottle to the twisted highway and listened to it shatter. "We need to make some headway before we run out of light."

Arthur finished his beer as Rabia made her way back to The Shark's cabin. He was going to throw his bottle too, and for a brief moment actually craved the chaos from it, but elected to gently place it on the ground instead. He then fought a terrible urge to mark the beers off the manifest.

Once back in The Shark, Rabia steered it back towards their destination: home. The road ahead of them, cracked and ill-gotten, twisted into the horizon like an endless golem turned snake. The Shark, despite whining initially, quickly became hungry for more concrete to tear into. With the immediate danger behind them, Arthur, drunk with love from his kiss with Rabia, allowed his intense curiosity to feed, picking up the giant tome that they had stolen.

Though he had opened it before to examine the bullet hole, he had not drunk in the misery and sorrow that the pages contained. Each page was meticulously written on in a very small and tightly packed margin. There was no date, but there were days, listed from one at the beginning going into the thousands. The sheer amount of people listed on a single page was overwhelming. The volume of human misery was staggering, and it was listed with the same cold-hearted apathy of a tax return. It was as if Arthur was staring into a mirror darkly, the methods of bureaucracy used to its zenith to buy and sell human souls. The man in Arthur wanted to scream while the number cruncher in him wanted to admire the handiwork.

The apathy scrolled across the pages for the crimes committed was more numbing than the number of people listed. There were names, with his own listed as the last, but most of the slaves were referred to as 'man', 'woman' or 'child'. As he looked at the half-empty page that held his name, he realized that he was only a quarter of the way through. The sociopathic ambition! That was the worst part, the fact that there were many, many more pages for The Colonel to fill with anally retentive business keeping.

If God was still alive, this would be the final nihilistic arrow that'd kill him for good.

Overwhelmed with empathy and sorrow, Arthur remembered what Rabia had said the day before.

"You bought a slave once?" he asked her.

"To set her free," Rabia said, defensively, keeping her eyes on the road.

"You helped them profit."

"To SET HER FREE, Arthur!" she repeated, hurt washing over her face.

He wasn't angry at her, he was just angry. He sat quietly for a minute, not daring to say anything more, afraid that he would say something undeserved. He returned his attention to the morbid book. He had ignored an important margin and was presently giving it the attention it deserved: *Client.* There were names here, but one came up again and again. On every page, *Main Client* appeared without fail. Whoever was buying these people by the bulk, they were responsible for the scale of The Colonel's operation. Somewhere out there, there was somebody *far worse* than the slavers.

Rabia parked the car off the road. Dusk was upon them. They were coming up to the dust plains with nothing on the horizon to hide them. She cleared her throat to get Arthur's attention. He jolted at the sound, coming back into the reality around him. He had become too immersed in the book to notice that they had come to a stop

"We camp here tonight," Rabia said, "we'll rotate sleep. There is nothing to hide us out here and I don't want to risk driving at night." With that, she got out of the car, refusing to look at Arthur.

"Her name was Melody," she said, hurt in her voice.

"You don't have to explain yourself—"

"I do. Please. I have told no one this since I left the caravan. She was beautiful, beautiful and sad. The Shepard forbade us to trade anything with slavers, but half of the cold-hearted bastard's sister wives were bought, so what the hell? I traded a rifle for her."

Rabia removed her sunglasses, revealing the hot tears they hid, swelling in her eyes. "So I brought her home. I don't think she actually liked me, though I hoped she would, I think she just stayed around those first couple of days to repay her freedom. The night she left, someone had caught us as naked as the day God spat us out. They went straight to the Shepard."

Arthur had never seen Rabia so vulnerable. He had hurt her with his accusation; it was just a question, the anger in it directed at his gruesome reading material, but the underlying message was *how dare you?* He felt like an asshole. "You are a good woman, Charlie Brown," he said, and Rabia smirked.

"The Shepard had never been able to read the bible that he touted at us," she continued, "but he claimed that what I had done was a terrible sin. There was no room in that maggot-infested mind of his for a black bi-sexual woman. Hell, there was no room in his mind for any type of queerness. By the time I had got my clothes on, Melody had fled, taking her freedom and my heart with her. By the time I had returned to my mother's rig, a dozen of the caravan's men were there with the caravan's Sheriff. The rules of the caravan were clear, my mother could give me up to them and their hungers, or she could give up her rig.

"A vehicle is everything in a caravan. It is a status symbol, a means of survival, and a home. Many had coveted her truck for as long as she had it. My mother gave it up to protect me, but I had earned her scorn. She never looked at me after that with anything but shame. She had agreed that I had sinned. I had found a new hell in the loss of my mother's affection."

There was distance between them, both physical and emotional. Arthur fought his instilled awkwardness and closed the gap. He embraced Rabia, holding her small frame and felt convulsions of silent crying shaking through it. She took a deep breath.

"One reason you don't trade with slavers," she went on, "besides the fact that no one should own another, is that you could go from customer to product quickly. They raided us in the night, having followed me back to my caravan. They were patient, they waited for days. When the hammer came down, my mother went up against a wall. She fought. The rifle I traded, my rifle, it was the one that did her in. Half of the caravan was taken or killed that night. All of it my fault. All because I was selfish enough to fall in love."

"I'm so sorry," said Arthur softly.

Rabia took a moment to gather her strength. She built up her composure and the serious, wry Rabia reappeared again. "We were too small in numbers to end them like I wanted, but I did the next best thing, I did what any patriot would do: I killed the Sheriff to take his rank, got the ugly swine bastards who took my mother's rig passed out drunk, and then castrated them in the night!"

"You're horrifying" Arthur said with less jest than before. "I'm sorry, I didn't mean to—"

"Don't apologize, this was cathartic. I've never had the chance to ravage slavers since then, so your plan to take this book, well, I could never repay you for the hell I got to bring down on them. I trust you, and that is something I felt was impossible in the United Wastes."

He expected her to move away from him, to either set up camp or fish out what little drugs she had left. Instead, her lips found his, and her hips pressed against his feverishly. He drew in her breath and felt her breasts heave on his chest. Her hands pulled his shirt out from his pants and moved their way underneath, finding the skin of his back. He reached for the fly of her shorts and she pushed him away, gently. She ran to The Shark and unpacked some blankets, which she threw to the floor then returned to his embrace.

Arthur moved his mouth over her neck and she wrapped her legs firmly around him. They raced to remove each other's clothes, exposing themselves to the cold temperature which had dropped significantly with the sun's light. But they found warmth in their union.

CHAPTER SEVENTEEN

If you want to avoid trouble, you don't drive at night.

Nocturnal predators have always been on the prowl.

When you drive at night, in the dead wasteland that sprawls across America, you are broadcasting yourself to every one of those predators. The roar of the engine in the otherwise coffin silence. The bright headlights like a lighthouse in the black of night. Movement, when there should be none. When you drive at night, you are screaming to be attacked. The only things awake at night are predators. *They* drive at night.

They drive at night because they are the ones doing the hunting...

...and there is always more than one way to pass a mountain.

CHAPTER EIGHTEEN

You can share your vulnerabilities with someone; you can share a sweaty act with them then lie naked and together; you can share this body and somehow walk away from it pleased and happy. But when all you have eaten is pre-war spam and instant mashed potatoes for days? Well, that function you need to do alone.

The drive for the past couple of days had been uneventful. No dust storms; no land pirates; no trouble, only the open road and the comfort of each other's eccentricities. The first day had disappeared behind them as quickly as the road, and the mountain and its inferno had become no more than a whiff of ash in the air. The second day was monotonous; it had felt like they were the last people on the planet as they drove for hours and hours witnessing no other signs of life. Given the death-scape of ruin around them, this may not have been far off.

Arthur knew that uneventful did not mean safe, but this kind of conclusion was all too easy to come to. That is not to say that they had not taken precautions though. Rabia had kept her weapons at the ready and Arthur had kept the book strapped to his back, just like the emaciated man, to make sure it did not leave their sight.

The abandoned and ruined concrete citadels that were once home to corporate empires rested empty and in view. They were just outside the deceased city's limits, and consequently outside the IRS boarders. Home was near; they only had to push a little bit further. Soon they would be in the safe confines of the bunker; soon they could deliver their bounty and set the monolithic gears of the last tax house into motion. Once this gargantuan beast had momentum behind it, an institution of slavery would crumble. Victory was so very near.

Arthur had to poop, and he had to do it out of view.

Reluctantly, Rabia parked The Shark and Arthur got out in a hurry. They were near an old strip mall, now stripped of its purpose. Rubble and decay had left most of this American staple in ruin, but the sturdy bank, the building nearest to The Shark stood intact.

"Where are you going?" Rabia asked as Arthur marched to the bank's door, its shattered glass no longer a barrier.

"Inside to find a toilet," he said, meekly.

"Just go out here!"

"Where you can see me?"

"I won't look," she said.

Arthur considered this not at all. "I've been going outside for days," Arthur reasoned. "I would like to use a toilet."

"So fucking what, G-Man! I've been going outside my entire life!" Rabia yelled.

Bowels in pain, Arthur ran inside. His movements were quick, but not natural. His legs were stiff and the book on his back forced him to arc forward. His one-shoed foot came with a slight hobble.

The interior of the bank was thick with dust from a generation's worth of no use. It caked off when touched, leaving a dryness in Arthur's throat and a layer on his shoeless foot. There were surprisingly few fully clothed skeletons, the remains of the pre-war civilians that had died here. Few clues were left to suggest the scavenging that had occurred. Paper money had been scattered about from the opened safe, likely left after the scavengers realized it could no longer feed them.

Arthur flew past the teller's counter and headed to the back. He found a small break room and an even smaller bathroom. Out of instinct, and a bashfulness that was borderline neurotic, Arthur shut the bathroom door behind him to hide his deed. He heard Rabia honk The Shark's horn and rolled his eyes at her impatience.

He flushed; the water went down but did not refill. He removed the toilet paper from its steel holding, knowing it was worth three times its weight in coffee back at the IRS bunker. Toilet paper and feminine hygiene products were like gold in the apocalypse. Before leaving the bathroom, he caught himself in the mirror. His carefully parted hair was tangled, almost matted, his white shirt grey from dirt and soot and blood caked to his skin. He smiled. "You did it," he said aloud. "You survived the suicide mission." Feeling much better having cleared himself out, he opened the bathroom door and walked out with a spring in his step.

But then he saw a pair of boots with decayed jaws on the toes. Something that once resembled pants webbed out from a codpiece. And a white three-piece suit and a hate symbol, not quite hidden by a grotesque, tumorous wattle.

A scornful and frightened Rabia Duke stood in front of The Colonel, her own shotgun digging into her back. The Colonel's sausage-like finger was on the trigger. Behind him stood the emaciated man, a chain and collar keeping him close.

He kept no doll.

"How 'bout you just mosey on over to your boyfriend over

there and I decide which one of you comes out alive and which one of you dies with my cock in their mouth." The Colonel pushed Rabia forward with the red shotgun.

"Try it and you leave without it, you Nazi douchenozzle," Rabia said, under her breath. She walked towards Arthur and stopped beside him. He was depressed to find that he could not see any one of the half-dozen or so weapons she normally kept on her person.

The Colonel pointed the shotgun at Arthur. "That book looks good on you, boy," he said, "How 'bout we keep it on you and you become my new table?" The eyes of the emaciated man grew at this, but he remained silent. The Colonel then pointed the shotgun at Rabia, "Or how 'bout you, missy? I'm sure you can improve my men's 'morale' issues they been havin' with those two pairs of lips of yours!" Rabia said nothing. When neither of the agents volunteered their opinions on their new job prospects, The Colonel licked his sausage of a finger and caressed his festering wattle.

This was it: the end of the line. Arthur had pushed his luck too far. The time he had borrowed now needed to be paid back with interest.

"I know why that book is so important to me," The Colonel said, "But why exactly is it so important to the IRS? It's just book keepin', nothin' inside of there is gonna give them the numbers of my men before they decide to raid." The Colonel blinked then threw the muzzle of the shotgun wildly towards Arthur. "That was *not* rhetorical, WHY IS MY BOOK SO IMPORTANT THAT YOU BURNT DOWN A THIRD OF MY BUSINESS FER IT?"

"Bookkeeping..." Arthur replied, fighting down the raw terror in his voice. "Bookkeeping is *the* most important thing to the IRS. We don't want to raid you; we want you to pay back taxes. You are the first establishment that the Internal Revenue Service has come across that has bothered to keep track of their sales. With it the first proper audit since The War can begin."

"Stop the horse shittin', boy," The Colonel said, "call it what it is. You plan on usin' it to raid me!"

"WE DON'T RAID!" Arthur yelled, surprising even Rabia. "We don't raid, it's called taxes and it's a good thing, GOD DAMMIT!"

The Colonel relaxed his finger on the trigger. "You know what, I'll bite, we been on the road just as long as you and my table over there ain't exactly the most entertaining man in the world. You convince me why your raiding is good and I'll let ya both go."

There was that terrible thing again: hope. The Colonel wet his fingers, had another quick round on his wattle and then pointed his nubby finger at Arthur. "Of course, if you don't, then you can choose which one of ya dies on your knees pleasin' me."

Rabia bared her teeth and bit the air, then nodded at Arthur, "You have a deal there, tumor dick," she said, nudging Arthur forward.

It looked at last as if everything fell on Arthur. It was up to him to save the day.

They were *fucked*.

"It's not stealing," Arthur began, "you pay a portion of your earnings to the government to keep it working."

"And why should I do that?" The Colonel queried.

"Because it is your duty as a patriot, as a—"

"Bullshit," The Colonel interjected. "I have a duty to myself and my business, so taking money from me keeps it out the pockets of my men."

"No, that's bullshit!" Arthur yelled, forgetting he was the one with the shotgun being pointed at. "You own slaves! Who exactly do you pay? Further, never in the history of ever has someone at the top shared their wealth, unless they were made to!"

The Colonel shifted his weight. "Hold up!" he said. "I ignored the fact that there was no government to pay these taxes to, I gave you the benefit of the doubt in your argument, so you can do the same for me!"

"Okay," said Arthur "I'll give you that, there being no government is a problem." He fought the urge to rant about how the other agencies of the federal government dropping the ball was not the IRS's fault (or problem), but let it go. "I can give you other reasons."

"Go on," said the Colonel. "Why should I pay taxes?"

"Because it pays for things that benefit you and your neighbor."

"Like what?"

"Like education, that can better the workforce and enlighten the next generation. Like health care that can be used to take care of your..." Arthur thought hard for an alternative to wattle. "...like your affliction. It can help pay for art and infrastructure, things that no one business or person could build on their own."

"Or bombs! Taxes is what paid for all this!" The Colonel said, motioning towards the ruin that was around them. "More than anything else, taxes paid for the bombs that we dropped and got dropped on us!"

"But it doesn't have to!" Arthur said, desperation scratching at his voice. "We can be better than that. Taxes are the cornerstone of a civilized world. We don't have to build bombs. We don't have to kill each other, or enslave each other, or worry about where our next meal will come from! We can all, each and every one of us, decide that the random cruelty we inflict on one another is akin to self-wounding. We can band together, make each other's lives better and pitch in with our wealth, knowing that it is an investment and a betterment of humanity. We can object to selfishness and personal wealth and instead give a portion of what we don't need to others. And we'd do this because it is right!"

Knees trembling, Arthur was holding back tears. The world had gone mad and no one seemed to care. If he could convince just one man, a leader of cruel men doing cruel things, that there were better things to strive for than their own needs, maybe there could be a change. Maybe it would all be worth it.

"Now why and the hell would I go and do somethin' like that? Did you just try and appeal to a man's moral center who kidnaps people, sells them as slaves, and just threatened to rape you before I killed you?"

"Well, I mean..." Arthur stuttered "Ah, well, when you put it that way, I suppose it was not a good argument."

"No shit, boy! Now, which one of you is going to die today?"

No hope now. Slavery might be worse than death, but Arthur could not bear to send Rabia to the grave. It was possible that she could fight her way out of slavery. Arthur was prepared to do the valiant thing and choose himself to die.

He began to step forward.

"I'll tell him!" Rabia yelled, pointing at the emaciated man. "I'll tell the god damn Colonel what you have been hiding from him you god damn swine bastard!"

"NO!" The emaciated man screamed back "Why would you do that? She's mine! He can't know!"

"I'll do it! I'll tell him what depravity you have been hiding, you god damn animal!"

"Shut up!" The emaciated man protested, rushing forward to silence Rabia. Murder was in his eyes. He was surprisingly fast for what little muscle was left hanging off of his bones. But his movement brought his leash taut and his momentum jerked The Colonel forward, forcing him to lose his balance. Rabia kicked the emaciated man in the face, sending him flying in another direction. This destroyed what little balance The Colonel still had and he fell to one knee, pinning the shotgun to the floor with his hand to steady himself. Rabia burst forward and leapt at The Colonel, stomping down on the hand over the shotgun, and like a rabid wolf sank her teeth deep into his wattle. The cry of pain from The Colonel was animalistic. As blood spilt onto Rabia's face she cupped The Colonel's balls and squeezed them like lemons. The Colonel opened his mouth as if he need to scream again but no howl came. She backed off quickly, then eyed Arthur and yelled "Run, G-Man! RUN, YOU BASTARD!"

The Colonel lay on the ground, clutching his genitalia as he squirmed like a fish above water. The emaciated man fumbled to his feet and rushed towards Rabia and Arthur as they fled, but clotheslined himself back to the floor once his leash was taut.

The book on Arthur's back made running hard, but he pounded the ground as much as physics would allow, not taking a moment to look back. Their fleeing caused dust to be kicked up into their mouths and Arthur thought that if death had a taste, that was it..

Soon, they were out of the bank and into the wastes once more. Arthur jetted towards The Shark, but Rabia yanked on his arm, pulling him in another direction. "He has the keys!" she said. "The guns too! Run like the bastard you are!"

The emaciated man flew out of the bank without The Colonel tugging at the leash. His chain ran down his neck and bounced on the ground as he fled towards his targets.

The emaciated man was fast for his condition. He scrambled quickly and closed the distance between them. "Wait! Take me with you!" he shouted.

Rabia stomped over and kicked him in the jaw again, sending him to the ground in a cloud of dust.

"What did you do *that* for?" Arthur berated, helping the skinny bastard up.

Rabia shrugged. "Old habits."

"I don't want to go back," the emaciated man said, tears mixing with nose blood. "I hate The Colonel."

"Speak of the devil!" said Rabia as The Colonel ran out the bank with the red shotgun in one hand, and his shattered balls in the other.

Letting go of his wounded jewels, The Colonel fired the gun. He hit nothing but his message was clear. Rabia, Arthur and the emaciated man ran and turned a corner around the bank.

The Colonel hobbled like he had a tunnel vision of thirsty revenge. He was much closer than Arthur was prepared for. The smell of dust and mildew-like aroma of dried bone marrow wafted upwards with each alarmed step. The grayness around them, caused from the years of decay of industrial construction, never meant for color in the first place, reflected light from the sun almost blindingly, as if the dust were newly fallen snow. The sound of pounding feet echoed off of the walls of the abandoned city, sounding like a cacophony of out of sync drums.

This went on for a full city block.

The roar of motorcycles rang against the walls of the ruined buildings. The Colonel's sled dogs were now on the prowl. If The Colonel didn't catch up with them, the motorcycles would.

Arthur's legs burned with lactic acid and his back tightened from the abuse of the giant book slamming into it with each step. He really wished he had both shoes. It looked to Arthur like Rabia was gritting her teeth as she ran.

The emaciated man looked mostly just confused.

The Colonel sprinted after them, not relenting for a moment.

The crunching of gravel and the low but powerful hum of engines grew closer.

All signs pointed to doom, except for one. Spray painted on a large particle board in the middle of the road about thirty yards away was a picture of a badge. A badge surrounding a scale and a solitary key. The official seal of the IRS. Behind that sign was the official border of the IRS, and with it the safety that came with well trained, ever vigilant snipers.

The finish line was well marked and the fanfare for those racing to it would erupt in gunfire. They just had to get there.

One shoe. A giant heavy book. Spent adrenaline. Chased by motorcycles. Yeah, they got this.

Arthur dared to look behind him, an urge that he could no longer fight. The motorcycles had turned the corner and now, with nothing attached to them or chaining them together, the riders moved at a killing speed. The Colonel was smiling.

Rabia picked up speed and raced towards the particle board. Arthur did his best to keep up, but was not nearly the athlete she was, despite her constant smoking.

Twenty yards away.

The sound of engines was excruciating.

Ten yards.

Arthur unfastened his employee badge from his shirt pocket and held it above his head. As they flew past the particle board, the motorcycles overtook them then slowed down and crossed in front, boxing them in.

"I am an IRS agent, Auditor #24, Arthur T. McDowell! Requesting assistance!" Arthur shouted as The Colonel's hand brushed his back.

The crack of gunfire rang out with thunderous authority.

The emaciated man's knee exploded in a mist of blood, and he fell to the ground screaming.

The IRS border snipers. Your taxpayer money hard at work.

"No no no! Not him, he's cool!" Arthur yelled at the hidden snipers. "I think, maybe. Did we decide that yet?" he asked a stunned Rabia, who responded with a shrug.

The Colonel stopped in his tracks as another crack of thunder rang into the air and chunks of pavement exploded up from a shot landing near his feet. His eyes spelt fury, his body sweaty, blood trickling down his horrendous wattle. The tyrant took a step backward.

"Yeah, that's the one!" Arthur yelled.

The electronic cackle of a loudspeaker conquered the air. "You are within IRS borders. Assaulting a federal agent of the United States Department of Treasury is a felony and will be dealt with immediately. Drop your weapon."

The Colonel dropped the shotgun and slowly stepped away.

The motorcycles parted and retreated behind The Colonel.

The emaciated man screamed in agony. Rabia gave The Colonel the bird with a wide, bloodstained smile.

"Listen here, boy," said The Colonel, "I'm not payin' no taxes, and if you come back to my place of business, you better believe that my primary client will be angry..." He instinctively touched his wattle, but winced in pain when he drew his chubby fingers down the hole Rabia had made. "... and my client is a son of a bitch like you have never seen."

"Get the fuck off of my lawn you grotesque chimp fucking bastard!" Rabia said as another warning shot was fired at The Colonel's feet.

The Colonel had been bested. The chase was over, but this? This was not walking away with your tail between your legs. This was going home to prepare for a bigger fight. The Colonel would no doubt have his revenge. He was patient, and not nearly dumb enough to try and cross the border to have it now. The Colonel stumbled backward then swung his heavy body over the motorcycle closest to him.

Rabia gave them the double bird, she looked over at Arthur with a wicked smile. He dropped his badge and joined her, bringing both of his hands up to join the vulgar gesture party. Watching a hateful bastard saunter off in defeat and not being the better man to him? This was victory.

The Colonel held on to the rider in front of him, and the motorcycles jerked forward before turning around. The slavers were leaving. Arthur was going home.

CHAPTER NINETEEN

The cold black and white checkered tiles of the bunker were spotless and clean. The concrete walls were without dust or stain.

This was a colossal problem.

As Arthur and Rabia made their way down to the office of Henry S. Boyd, who was now a full commissioner, there was not a single flaw that Arthur could spot on the walls or floor. It had not just been cleaned methodically, but hand scrubbed to the molecule. It was almost beautiful if it did not portend doom for the one cleaning. Whoever had done this job, if they kept it up, was in direct line of sight for a promotion into auditing.

That's when he saw her.

Merely a few yards past the door that Arthur was about to enter was the little girl he had saved from the suburbs and from being eaten by Murder-Man. She was in coveralls that were a size too big for her, pushing along a cart carrying cleaning supplies that were taller than her. It was comical looking at the little one labor to move something that was never designed with her in mind. Almost. The fact of the matter was this: she was doing her job *too* well.

Arthur and Rabia looked like the hell they had just been through and subsequently waged. The new Commissioner wanted to see them immediately, with an appointment set a mere ten minutes after they had arrived, which was so prompt it was almost unheard of. Arthur's tie and shoe were missing, Rabia's shirt stained in The Colonel's blood; neither looked as professional as the words across Rabia's hat suggested.

Arthur paused at the door.

Protocol had kept him from warning the little girl before. He wanted desperately to tell her days ago that she should slack off, perpetually enjoy her position and never stand out. She was only a table away then, but the social contract of the IRS was clear: eat with your own kind and keep your head down. So he did nothing. He did nothing, and in the span of a week the damage had been done.

Arthur raised his hand to knock on the door, but froze in midair.

Arthur McDowell had followed protocol to the letter his entire life, breaking it only recently to 'fraternize' with Rabia. How important was keeping up with these bureaucratic standards really? At the end of the day, wasn't what the IRS had been trying to accomplish since nuclear annihilation a Sisyphean task? Hadn't the very system he had been championing his entire life purposefully sent him to his death to cover for the throne-taking of the commissioner's office?

Wasn't his warning worth being slightly late for?

Arthur lowered his hand.

She did not see him at first, her line of sight blocked by the cleaning cart that she was pushing. Arthur cleared his throat and she either did not hear him or did not recognize the gesture. It was not until the cart had gently bumped into

Arthur that she looked to see what had blocked its passage.
The tiniest, faintest smile graced her face upon recognizing
him. It was likely the most she had ever smiled. "Hello," she
said, meekly, "can you move?"

"No," said Arthur. "Not yet. There is something important I need to tell you."

The little girl blinked in response.

"You are doing a good job," he said.

"Thank you!" she replied with a smile.

"No. No, that just won't do. You are doing *too* good a job.
Do you understand?"

"No."

"Okay, so it's like this: people around here who do well,
they get promoted, which means they get to do other jobs,
but you don't want those other jobs. Those other jobs are
scary and dangerous, and it means you will have to work
outside."

After hearing the word 'outside', the little girl's eyes
widened in terror, but a lifetime of fear meant that she otherwise kept her composure.

"I did a great job wherever they put me," Arthur said,
"and you know what happened? They rewarded people who
skated by and my job always got worse. Only those evil
enough to want power, or who are lazy enough to not care,
excel in this environment. They need those like us to work
hard so they have someone to take credit from. Don't get
noticed or they'll attach themselves to you, do you
understand?"

The little girl nodded.

"This will be the most important advice that you will ever
get in an office job like this, and because this is the only office
left on the planet I need you to promise me that you will
never try hard," Arthur pleaded.

"I promise," the little girl said.

"Good," said Arthur, relieved.

The little girl moved past him now, at a greatly reduced speed. Once she was past him, Arthur checked the time. He was two minutes late.

"That was some good advice, I guess," Rabia said, patting Arthur on the shoulder. "Not sure if I would approve if I hadn't seen this place with my own eyes."

"It's the advice I wish someone gave me after my dad died, but I didn't realize I felt half of what I said until a couple of days ago," he replied.

The two agents, covered in grime, dirt, blood, and unwashed sex, opened the door to Boyd's office. They immediately stood out among the insane order and cleanliness within. All of Boyd's cabinets had been moved to this new larger office, yet because it was twice the size of the old one, they had filled only half the room. The spaces they hadn't filled were measured out in a grid of blue painter's tape, each rectangle that they outlined signifying an exact space for another cabinet to be installed. Through habit and nervousness, Arthur made to straighten his tie but when he was reminded it was no longer there, he awkwardly moved his hand up to his chin and rubbed his newly grown stubble.

The grandfather clock-like face of Mr. Boyd looked more than sullen, it looked offended. There was a ruler in his hand to, as ever, regularly measure out the distance between his monitor and his coffee. The sight of the mug stirred anger inside of Arthur. The image of the red-haired agent decapitated and placed on a pike, who had failed to fill Boyd's cup quickly enough that day, hung in his mind like a terrible hangover. In the span of their last conversation, Henry S. Boyd had drunk three cups, more than Arthur could afford to have in a month. There was apparently never a shortage of coffee; whatever they had rationed away was plenty to keep those high up nice and happy. But this was no longer a prized status symbol to Arthur. It was a symbol of greed and abused power.

It also probably had too much sugar in it.

"You're late!" Boyd barked.

"I know," replied Arthur, "and I don't care." Rabia stood to the side, hands behind her back, but with a posture and demeanor too relaxed to be respectful. She smiled at Arthur's rebellion.

Boyd looked at Arthur long and hard. He did not drink down half of his coffee, as he would have done without this offense, nor did he reprimand, because no one had ever been late and not apologized. He simply did not have the toolkit for this. After a pregnant moment of passive aggressiveness between the two men (and stifled giggles from Rabia) Boyd continued.

"That, ah, abomination you are wearing is a current and up to date bookkeeping ledger I hear?" he said, and then downed half of his coffee.

"Yes sir," Arthur said with no love for the man he was speaking to.

"Don't get me wrong, Mr. McDowell, something like this is highly coveted," Boyd said. We have not been able to go over the business records of any organization since the bombs dropped because no one has kept any. With it we can seize back taxes and that is incredibly valuable, but it is not what you were sent out to get. Can I assume that you have your completed census forms?"

"Mr. Boyd, this abomination doubles as my census efforts. I challenge any other agent to supply a census as thoroughly written as this, because the product being sold by the organization that I seized this from is people. It lists their race, age, gender and even the location of their buyers. There is no better record of the population west of here, guaranteed, and it will allow us the opportunity to strengthen the government's current surplus once auditing and collection efforts begin." Arthur unbuckled the book from his back, releasing the smell of wet leather. He stepped toward the desk and dropped the tome with no regard for its weight or the sanctity of Boyd's anal measuring. It landed on the desk with thunderous bass. Rabia's smile turned into a Cheshire cat snarl.

Stunned at first, the Commissioner turned the pages of the book slowly. His eyes grew wider with each page. "This is...astounding," he said. He kept turning pages, revealing person after person and asset after asset. Horror did not grace Boyd's face as it had Arthur's when he read it. Alarmingly, his reactions suggested hunger rather than horror. "Incredible work," he whispered, then met the eyes of Arthur. "I suppose I can forgive lateness for something like this. You have gone above and beyond, like always," Boyd then said something that would have made Arthur's heart sing only days ago, but now filled him with murky contempt: "Good job."

The Commissioner raised his mug to kill the other half of coffee when his door suddenly opened. A woman, white shirt, black tie and black skirt marched into the office with a fresh mug of coffee, but froze mid-stride. Arthur's tardiness had interrupted the schedule of the coffee. She was on time, but without the other mug finished had nothing to carry back. She set the mug on the desk without collecting the one in Boyd's hand. She then pivoted, walked to the door, signed that her job was complete, and then left. Boyd looked somehow wounded.

Rabia cleared her throat in a way that was both vulgar and demanding. Boyd looked up at her, holding his half-empty mug impotently. "Ah, well, yes, a good job to you too," he said. "You kept our man safe, and I am sure that your role in this was substantial."

"I did ninety percent of the work sir," she said in a half-muffled voice. Arthur did not protest.

"Well ah, good," Boyd replied, still not sure if he should drink both and measure them, or drink one and measure, then drink the other and measure. "This was more than enough to grant you a full-time contract and residence with the IRS. Good work," he said in a near whisper, still deciding how to deal with his chaos.

"Thank you for the promotion sir," Rabia said. "Does this mean that I get the employee discount?"

Boyd nodded his head. He then drank from the mug in his hand and picked up the new mug with his other, electing to just hold both of them.

There was nothing left to be said. Well, at least not by Boyd. Arthur stayed where he was, relishing the wasted time that expired as he refused to leave.

"Sir?" he said.

"Oh ah, yes, that's right," Boyd stumbled, "You were promised a promotion. Ah, well, I am sorry to say that it was filled while you were gone..."

"You gave it to Ralph Siemens," Arthur said.

"Yes, er, that's right. How did you know?"

"Dewitt told me."

Color drained from Boyd's face. He shuffled in his seat and cleared his throat. He sounded scared. Arthur did not think that Henry S. Boyd was capable of guilt, but fear? Oh yes.

Oh yes indeed.

Before Boyd could say anything, the office door opened once more and a man with a white shirt, black tie and black slacks walked in with another mug of coffee. The same snap decision that the woman made was made by him, and he placed the new mug on Boyd's desk, leaving him with three mugs to juggle. Rabia and Arthur took this as an opportunity to leave.

The agents angled towards the door, not wanting to be excused. Boyd was too busy dealing with his coffee nightmare and the knowledge that Arthur knew his predecessor's fate. The book they had delivered put things in motion that even Henry S. Boyd, with all of his new found power was helpless to stop. On paper, it was simple: the IRS was going to audit a business. The reality was far grimmer: the IRS was going to war.

It would be the first one fought since the Intercontinental Ballistic Missiles had their day out in the sun.

What Boyd had said to Arthur when all of this began was true, but in a way that neither man could foresee. A new dawn for the IRS had broken.

Rabia left the room, knowing her, eager for a cigarette, and presumably to check out her new accommodations. Arthur was happy for her. Much of what she had just earned he had taken for granted. She was a strong self-made woman, and he was proud to know her.

Arthur paused at the door, and then turned around.

"Sir?" he said.

The Commissioner's eyes were still wide, puppy like. His hands were full, not knowing how to solve his dilemma. He looked up at Arthur, and for the first time he looked vulnerable. "Yes?" he said.

"It can be a secret, you know," Arthur said. "Dewitt asked me to do something, but I would have to go out of my way as it's not my department. I am still at heart a bureaucrat, so I probably won't do it, unless you give me a reason."

The politics had changed. Boyd was unprepared for it.

"Of course, I understand," he uttered with a nod, frantically looking from one coffee mug to the next.

"When you mobilize our efforts to seize The Colonel's assets," Arthur said. "You put me on the front lines."

Get Memos from the Wasteland FREE!

Bleakly funny in all of the wrong places, *Memos From The Wasteland* contains five short stories from the United Wastes. Letters, **Rabia's gonzo diary**, memos and office tiffs paint a bitter picture where bureaucracy still reigns.

Get your free copy at https://revfitz.com!

CONTAINS "ACTIVITIES".

ABOUT THE AUTHOR

M.P. Fitzgerald lives in Seattle and is dedicated to injecting the feverish Gonzo style into fiction. He is an author, illustrator, and an amateur mad scientist. He has authored the *Existential Terror and Breakfast* series, *The Nihilist's Horoscope* (which is free), and is writing the next book in *The Happy Bureaucracy* series.

The author greatly appreciates you taking the time to read his work. Please consider leaving a review wherever you bought the book, or telling your friends about it to help spread the word.

Connect with M.P. Fitzgerald
Website: https://revfitz.com
Email: contact@revfitz.com

Made in the USA
Monee, IL
28 December 2020